"I'd like us to try to maintain separate lives as much as possible. In all respects."

Meggie just looked at him for a moment. "But why?"

Cavan tossed his pen onto the desk. "Look, Meghan, this marriage has gotten off to a rocky start. I think that until we figure out what we're going to do with each other, we ought to maintain a respectable distance."

"I thought we were. I mean, one kiss in four weeks of marriage isn't exactly living on intimate terms."

Cavan smiled. "You cut right through to the basics, don't you?"

"I've found that it saves time, and I'd appreciate it if you'd do the same."

"All right. I want to make sure that we don't ruin our chances for an anullment."

Her heart caught. "I see. Why don't you want to sleep with me, Cavan?"

"I do want to Meghan. That's the problem."

Dear Reader,

Welcome to Silhouette. Experience the magic of the wonderful world where two people fall in love. Meet heroines who will make you cheer for their happiness, and heroes (be they the boy next door or a handsome, mysterious stranger) who will win your heart. Silhouette Romances reflect the magic of love—sweeping you away with books that make will you laugh and cry, heartwarming, poignant stories that will move you time and time again.

In the next few months, we're publishing romances by many of your all-time favorites, such as Diana Palmer, Brittany Young, Emilie Richards and Arlene James. Your response to these authors and other authors of Silhouette Romances has served as a touchstone for us, and we're pleased to bring you more books with Silhouette's distinctive medley of charm, wit and—above all—*romance*.

I hope you enjoy this book and the many stories to come. Experience the magic!

Sincerely,

Tara Hughes
Senior Editor
Silhouette Books

BRITTANY YOUNG
Gallagher's Lady

Silhouette Romance

Published by Silhouette Books New York

America's Publisher of Contemporary Romance

SILHOUETTE BOOKS
300 E. 42nd St., New York, N.Y. 10017

Copyright © 1986 by Brittany Young

ISBN: 0-373-08454-4

First Silhouette Books printing September 1986

America's Publisher of Contemporary Romance

Printed in the U.S.A.

BRITTANY YOUNG

lives and writes in Racine, Wisconsin. She has traveled to most of the countries that serve as the settings for her Romances and finds the research into the language, customs, history and literature of these countries among the most demanding and rewarding aspects of her writing.

IRELAND

North Channel

NORTHERN IRELAND

Donegal

Belfast

Donegal Bay

Sligo

Carrick-on-Shannon

ATLANTIC OCEAN

REPUBLIC OF IRELAND

Galway

Dublin

Galway Bay

River Shannon

IRISH SEA

Shannon Airport

Limerick

Killarney

Waterford

Dingle Bay

River Lee

Cork

Kinsale

CELTIC SEA

N
W E
S

Chapter One

Meghan Kathleen O'Neill raced her horse along the narrow road, her slender body moving as one with the large stallion. Wind whipped her long, auburn hair behind her. It was such a joy to be out of that stuffy boarding school and back in the Irish countryside where she belonged.

Suddenly a car sped around the curve at almost the same time as Meggie, only in the opposite direction. The frightened stallion, who had been running all out, stopped dead in his tracks, rearing on his hind legs and twisting until Meggie lost her grip and hit the ground behind him with a thud. Stunned, she watched helplessly as the stallion raced off into the distance, a close second to the car that hadn't bothered to stop.

Another car stopped next to Meggie and the man driving quickly got out to help. "Are you all right?"

From her vantage point on the ground, her eyes wandered up over long, muscled legs and a lean torso, finally coming to rest on a dark, unconventionally handsome face she'd never seen before. "I've been better, I must say." She started to sit up, but winced at a pain in her shoulder. "Much better."

"Stay still." The stranger pressed her gently back to the ground. "Where are you hurt?"

"My shoulder mostly, and my arm a little."

He firmly probed her arm with his fingers. Warm, gentle fingers. Meggie stared at the top of his dark head, more interested in him than her shoulder. "Are you a doctor?" she asked in her delightful musical accent.

"No."

"Then what are you doing?"

"You don't need a medical degree to know when a bone is broken." He helped her into a sitting position. "Lift your sweater."

Meggie's eyes twinkled despite the pain in her shoulder. "It's a bit soon in our relationship, don't you think?"

For the first time his eyes looked directly into Meggie's, and she was struck by their intense shade of blue. And she was struck by something else; the deep-rooted anger that emanated from him, as though he carried it with him always. He couldn't have been more than twenty-six, yet he seemed much older.

Without another word, Meggie turned her back to him and lifted her sweater. Again his fingers gently probed, and again Meggie was aware of their warmth—until he found a tender spot. She inhaled sharply and shot him a look over her shoulder as he lowered her sweater. "I don't mean to state the obvious, but ouch."

"Nothing is broken, but you have a bad bruise and some swelling. I think you should go to the hospital."

"What would they do to me there?"

"Pack it in ice, probably."

"I can do that myself."

He got to his feet and held out a hand to help her up. As Meggie brushed off her jeans using the arm that didn't hurt, she stared unabashedly up at him. He apparently felt her gaze and leveled his eyes at her once more. "If you have something to say, say it."

Meggie straightened, her composure unruffled. She liked people and people usually liked her. But not this fellow. "Actually, I was expecting you to say something to me about the way I was riding."

He shook his head. "If you want to commit suicide by behaving recklessly on a public road, that's your business. But I think you should show a little more consideration for your horse."

"There," she smiled with satisfaction. "Don't you feel better for getting it out of your system? And it happens that I agree with you. Even though this road is rarely used, it was reckless of me to ride like that."

He said nothing.

Meggie tilted her head to one side. "You're not the friendliest person I've ever met."

Again he said nothing, but Meggie was no quitter.

"I don't think I've seen you around here before. Everyone in the town knows everyone else. Are you just passing through?"

"I was, until about ten minutes ago."

"Ah, he speaks."

At that, a corner of the man's mouth lifted. "Are you always like this?"

"Like what?"

"Like a five-foot, three-inch leprechaun, spreading good cheer wherever you go."

"I never thought of myself quite like that. You're American, aren't you?"

"Yes."

"Yet there's something vaguely Irish about you. Are your ancestors from Ireland?"

"My grandparents."

She nodded her auburn head knowingly. "I see. So you're here to discover your heritage."

"A nosy, cheerful leprechaun. What a combination."

Meggie smiled and a delightful dimple creased her cheek. "Could I ask you for a small favor?"

The dark-haired man had warmed up considerably. He found her to be completely charming. "You will anyway."

Meggie didn't quite know why, but she didn't want him to go yet, and something told her he'd be off in a few minutes if she didn't think of something to hold him there. "Would you mind giving me a lift home? It's rather a long walk from here."

"It would serve you right for riding your horse that way."

Meggie just looked at him with hopeful hazel eyes.

"Yes," he said in resignation, "I'll give you a ride."

"Thank you," she said with a quick smile. "For a minute I thought you might leave me standing here."

"You have good instincts."

"Yes, I do." Her smile faded a little. There was something about him...something in him that touched her. She couldn't begin to explain it, but she knew that this man was somehow going to play an important role in her life. They were standing near his sports car. Meggie stretched a friendly hand across the low roof. "By the way, my name is Meghan O'Neill."

The eyes he leveled at her when she spoke her name sent a chill down her spine.

Meggie slowly retracted her hand until it fell to her side. "Why are you looking at me like that?"

He ignored her question. "Are you any relation to Padraic O'Neill?"

"I'm his granddaughter. Do you know him?"

"We've met," he said tersely. "Get in." He climbed into the car and started the engine. Meggie quickly hopped into the passenger seat. Almost before she closed the door, he had slammed the little car into gear and turned it around.

"I live..."

"I know where you live."

"There's no need to snap at me. I had no way of knowing that." She frowned at him. "Who are you?"

"Gallagher. Cavan Gallagher."

"Cavan Gallagher," she repeated thoughtfully as she settled into her seat. "That sounds familiar." As soon as the words were out, Meggie realized where she'd heard the name. There had been a Cavan Gallagher who, seven years earlier, had a summer job in the stables at a neighbor of her grandfather's named Farrell. One day it was discovered that a small fortune in jewels had been stolen from Mrs. Farrell and they were found in this Cavan Gallagher's cottage. He had been tried for theft, found guilty and sent to prison.

Cavan glanced at her sideways and saw from her face that she remembered. "I am who you think," he said quietly, his jaw taut. "Would you still like a lift home or would you rather I stopped the car so you can walk?"

Meggie stared at his profile. "I'll stay where I am, thank you." She was quiet for a few minutes. "Did you do it?" she suddenly asked.

"Does it matter?"

"Of course it does."

He glanced over at her and then looked back at the road. "I don't feel any need to explain myself to a teenager I've never met before."

"Well, you certainly put me in my place, didn't you?" The way she said the words made it sound like a simple matter-of-fact remark. There was no resentment.

Cavan turned his head and their eyes met. Hers were so clear and open. She had no idea of the full story of what had happened to him, or of the role her family had played in it. He turned his attention back to the road and a long silence fell between them. "No," he suddenly said.

Meggie looked at him curiously. "No?"

"No, I didn't do it."

Meggie didn't know why she believed him, but she did. Or, more importantly, why it should matter to her—but it did. "I'm glad."

"Why?"

Hazel eyes looked into blue. "Because I like you," she said quietly. "Though I don't for the life of me know why. It certainly isn't your charm."

Her remark caught Cavan off guard, and he laughed. He couldn't remember the last time he'd laughed.

As he turned the car onto the long drive that led to the elegant Tudor mansion where she lived, she pointed toward the stables. "Look. My horse made it back before me."

"Do you ride a lot?"

"As much as I can when I'm here on vacation. I'm away at school most of the year."

"College?"

"Boarding school," she said in disgust. "College is next year." As Cavan stopped the car in front of her house, Meggie tried to think of a way to keep him there longer. "Can I invite you in for some tea or coffee? Our customs around here are mostly American because my grandfather lived there for a while himself, so you'd be quite comfortable."

"No, thank you. I'm not what you'd call a sought-after guest in these parts."

"Then why did you come back?"

What could he tell her? That he had a few scores to settle—including one with her grandfather? "No more questions, Meghan O'Neill. This is where you get out."

A strange knot formed in Meggie's stomach. She didn't want him to go, but there was no way to keep him there any longer. She climbed out of the car, but looked in the window. "Thank you for your help, Cavan."

He looked at her for a long moment. "You're welcome. Goodbye."

Meggie backed away from the car and watched as Cavan drove away. Her grandfather came out of the house and stood next to her. "I'm glad to see you're all right. I was a little concerned when I saw your horse come home alone."

"I fell off."

"Who was that man who brought you home?"

"Cavan Gallagher."

Meggie was still watching Cavan's car so she didn't see the way her grandfather's face paled. "What's he doing in Kilgarrin?"

Meggie turned to look at her grandfather. "He didn't say, specifically. He did, however, mention that he knew you."

Her grandfather didn't say anything.

"Grandfather? Do you remember him at all? He was the man accused of taking Mrs. Farrell's jewelry—"

"I know who he is, Meggie," he cut her off short. "And I don't want you seeing him any more."

"There's not much chance of that. I expect he's going back to America." She looked at him curiously. "You don't like him, do you, grandfather?"

"He's been in prison."

"For something he didn't do."

"You know that after one meeting?"

"Without question." She looked back down the drive, but Cavan's car was long out of sight. "He wasn't pleased when I told him who I was. Did the two of you have a run-in?"

"Mr. O'Neill!" a maid called from the door. "You have a phone call."

"Excuse me, Meggie."

She nodded, still staring down the road. Cavan Gallagher was gone, and Meghan Kathleen O'Neill was filled with such a sense of loss that she ached with it. Nothing like this had ever happened to her before. She didn't understand it and while it frightened her more than a little, it also felt rather good.

Meggie thought of Cavan Gallagher often during the following years, not realizing until much later what had happened to her in so short a time.

Chapter Two

Five years later.

Mist shrouded the ancient Irish cemetery as the sun prepared to set behind the stone church nearby. Meggie walked among the tombstones, her full calf-length skirt swishing in the silence. As she paused for a moment beside the newly dug grave of Alastair Farrell, her nose wrinkled just a little at the musty smell of the freshly dug earth combined with the sweet scent of the wilted cut flowers.

Meggie's hazel eyes gazed around the neatly kept grounds as she rubbed her hands on her arms to generate some warmth on this cool Irish evening. She knew nearly all of the markers by heart. Many of them were more than three hundred years old. Others, their carvings smoothed to near invisibility from centuries of weather, were said to be older.

Alastair's death had set something off inside Meggie. For five years now, off and on, thoughts of Cavan Gallagher had haunted her. She would have expected that the memory of a single encounter that happened when she was eighteen would have faded, but it hadn't. And tonight, for the first time since then, she had a feeling that he was near. Meggie's sigh gently ruffled the air as she pushed her heavy auburn hair away from her face. But where?

"Meggie, what are you doing out here at this hour?"

Meggie inhaled sharply and turned to find her grandfather coming down the path toward her. "Oh, it's you! You startled me," she said with a relieved smile. "I wasn't expecting you."

"I just came out to wish a final farewell to old Alastair. He could be a mighty unpleasant man at times, but I'll miss him nonetheless." He glanced down at his granddaughter. "I don't expect you're here for the same reason, are you, Meggie?"

"No," she answered quietly, without elaboration, as her gaze went beyond the stone fence that surrounded the quiet grounds. "Grandfather, do you think it's possible to fall in love with someone after only one meeting, and still be in love with that person years later?"

He looked at her curiously, wondering to whom she was referring. "I do, Meggie. It doesn't happen to many people, but it does happen."

A thoughtful silence fell between them as they strolled down the grassy path to a large but simple monument that marked the final resting place of members of the O'Neill family. Meggie ran her fingertips over the cool, smoothly polished granite, tracing the carved names of her father and mother. "How does one live with something like that?" Meggie finally asked.

"Day by day. Month by month. Year by year."

Meggie looked at him with interested hazel eyes. "It sounds as though you've suffered through the same sort of thing."

He reached out a gentle hand and cupped the face of this young woman who was so dear to his heart. "It seems to be the fate of the O'Neills to suffer from unrequited love. Sometimes you have to settle for something other than what you want."

"I won't ever settle." Her eyes rested on the tombstones of her parents. "Life is too short to spend it with someone you can never truly love."

"Ah, you're thinking about Alastair's grandson Sean."

"I told you a long time ago that I'm not going to marry him."

This was one of the few subjects the two of them disagreed about with any vehemence. "It was your father's wish, Meggie. He contracted for your marriage to Sean before he died."

"Grandfather, that's emotional blackmail and you know it. I'm not in love with him."

"Love will grow during marriage. You might not love him now, but you could learn to. Your grandmother and I did. Granted, she wasn't the grand passion of my life, but I did love her in my way."

Meggie didn't say anything.

"Meggie?"

"I'm sorry." Her voice filled with genuine regret. "I hate to disappoint you, but this is something I simply can't do."

"Your older sister married Sean's brother, just the way she was supposed to. Just the way your father decided."

"Caroline always does what she's told. I only do what I'm told if I happen to agree with it."

At that, the old man relented and laughed, reaching out to catch Meggie in a bear hug. "So you do, and so you always have. I hate to admit it, but that's one of the things I love best about you. Makes you a bit difficult to live with at times, though."

He held her away from him, his smile fading. "We'll talk about this marriage with Sean another time. It has to be settled. You're twenty-three and he's twenty-five. His father tells me that Sean's getting tired of waiting for you to set a date."

"Sean is, he says? We both know better than that, don't we, Grandfather? Sean doesn't want to marry me any more than I do him. We're more like brother and sister than husband and wife."

"So what do you suggest I tell Hugh Farrell?"

"That he find someone else to prey on," she answered lightly.

"That's a terrible thing to say."

"Terrible, but true. We both know that the only reason he wants me in his family is because of the money I can bring him and the luster of my family tree."

Her grandfather knew she was right, but he still couldn't just let it slide. The family honor was on the line. "We'll talk about this more tomorrow. Right now I'm late getting up the hill to Father Flaherty for our game of chess. Don't stay out here too long, dear, or you'll catch a chill."

"I won't." Then she remembered something. "Oh, Grandfather, did you return John's call from O'Neill Textiles?"

"I did. That's why I'm late."

"He sounded upset when I spoke with him. What was wrong?"

"It seems there's another textile factory crowding our market. Our sales have gone down unbelievably in the past few months."

"Do you know who it is?"

"For all the good the knowledge will do me. It's an outfit called AmeriTextiles. They make basically the same things we do, but they manage to sell them for less. A lot less. I don't know how they can make a profit."

"And your customers are going over to Ameri-Textiles?"

"One by one." He shook his head. "I don't know, Meggie. I'm a little worried." Then he smiled at her. "Listen to me going on when I should be playing chess. Don't concern yourself with any of this. It'll all work itself out. It always does. But you and Sean Farrell—that's another matter entirely."

Meggie's quick smile touched her eyes. "You don't give up easily, do you, Grandfather?"

"Not about this." He waved over his shoulder as he walked away from her. As Meggie's eyes followed him down the path her smile faded. She loved her grandfather dearly. In the years since her parents had died, he had always been there for her. And now not only did he have to worry about a business that wasn't going well, he was disappointed in his granddaughter because she wouldn't marry the man she was supposed to.

Again Meggie's gaze wandered beyond the stone wall. Where was Cavan Gallagher?

A tall man with black hair stood perfectly still in the doorway of the pub, his blue eyes narrowed as he peered through the haze of smoke at the faces in the room. They suddenly narrowed even more as they came to rest on the sandy head of a man at a far table studying the poker hand that had just been dealt to him.

Cavan strode forward and stood directly across the table from the man, his gaze never leaving him, and waited. The three other men at the table shifted uneasily in their chairs at the cold anger that emanated from the stranger until finally they threw their cards on the table and left, unwilling to get into the middle of whatever was about to happen.

The sandy-haired man raised his eyes at last and stared at Cavan expressionlessly. "Do I know you?"

"You should. You helped the O'Neills frame me for the theft of your mother's jewels."

Hugh Farrell's eyes narrowed, but there was an alertness about his suddenly tense body. "I don't know what you're talking about."

Cavan reached into the inside pocket of his jacket and removed a bundle of notes that he tossed onto the table in front of Hugh.

"What are these?"

"Read them, Hugh. It'll save us both a lot of time."

One by one he picked them up and read them, then threw them back on the table and leaned cockily back in his chair, his hands behind his head. "So? You're holding some notes on money my father borrowed."

"You should learn to read things more carefully, Hugh. I bought these notes from the men your father owed money. Alastair is dead now and you owe the money. You owe it to me. Failing payment in full within twenty-four hours, you'll be served with papers forcing the sale of your home, your land and anything on that land, including the horses. Sixty percent of the money your belongings earn at auction will be paid to me."

As Cavan spoke, Hugh sat up straighter and straighter and looked through the notes again. "My father would never have borrowed that kind of money. His pride wouldn't have allowed him to."

"Thanks to your gambling, his need was apparently greater than his pride." Cavan's voice was deep and soft, but there was an edge of steel to it. "There is, however, an alternative to selling off your property."

"I'm listening."

"A wager. Each of us will draw one card. Whoever gets the high card wins everything. And I mean everything, including the marriage contract you hold for your son on the O'Neill girl. And if I win, you'll sign a paper stating that you played a part in framing me for the theft of the jewels."

"Wait just a minute. I don't mind wagering for the land and the debt, but as far as signing what amounts to a confession, I don't think so. I could be the one who ends up in prison."

"I only want to clear my name and that's what I intend to use it for."

"I don't know." Hugh shook his head. "And the contract..."

Hugh was a risk-taker, but that contract was a large piece of his security. Meggie would bring the family a lot of money and prestige, especially now that his oldest son, Tom, was dead, leaving Meggie's sister Caroline free to marry again.

"Not the contract, and not the confession."

Cavan just looked at him for a long moment with such cold hatred that it chilled Hugh. Then he walked away.

Hugh blankly watched him for a moment, then came to his senses.

"Wait a minute! Where are you going?"

Cavan turned. "I have better things to do than play games with you. You either bet it all, or nothing. There's no in-between."

"Look, I can understand why you want the signed confession, but what's so important to you about the bloody marriage contract?"

Cavan walked back, pressed his hands flat on the table and leaned toward Hugh. "Because," he said with a deadly quiet, "I intend to strip you of everything you hold dear. You want the O'Neill girl's money and I intend to see that you don't get it. But more importantly, she's Padraic O'Neill's granddaughter."

"In other words, if I don't sign the confession, and offer the marriage contract as part of the wager, all bets are off."

"Exactly.

"You leave me no choice."

Hugh tossed back a shot of whiskey. "Very well, Gallagher. You want to play an all-or-nothing game so that's what we'll play. New deck. I get the first cut."

Cavan took the seat directly across the table from Hugh. A circle of people gathered silently around to watch the drama unfolding. One man handed Hugh a deck of cards, the seal on the box unbroken. Another got a shot glass for Cavan and poured him a whiskey, then refilled Hugh's glass. Cavan seemed not to notice. His attention was focused entirely on the man across from him as Hugh broke the seal and shuffled the deck. Hugh set the deck in the middle of the table and took the first cut, saying a silent prayer as he looked at his bottom card, and then smiling and holding up the queen of hearts for all to see.

Cavan took a cut and laid it face-up on the table without even looking at it for several seconds, but knowing from the sound of the crowd that he'd won. He usually did.

Hugh gazed in horror at the ace of spades Cavan had drawn as Cavan lifted his whiskey glass in a half salute and drank it in one swallow. His eyes still on Hugh, Cavan set the glass firmly on the table and rose. "I'll expect you, your wife and any other Farrells to be out of the house and off of the property in one week."

Cavan stopped next to Hugh's chair and looked down at him without sympathy. "You should never gamble what you can't afford to lose," he said quietly, and then left.

Hugh leaned back in his chair. His arms hung limply by his sides. What had he done?

Padraic O'Neill sat behind his massive desk sifting through old correspondence.

"Mr. O'Neill?"

He looked up to find a uniformed maid standing in the doorway.

"There is a man here to see you. He says it's important."

"What's his name?"

"Cavan Gallagher."

The old man paled, but his voice was strong. "Send him in."

"He's already in," Cavan said as he entered from behind the maid and walked across the long room to take a seat across the desk.

Padraic's eyes locked with Cavan's. "Close the doors, Ginny."

When the maid had gone, the old man spoke. "What are you doing here?"

"I've come for your granddaughter," Cavan said evenly.

"Caroline might be widowed, but I seriously doubt if she'd be interested in the likes of you."

"She was once. Enough to run off with me. But this time I'm not referring to Caroline. I'm here for Meghan."

Padraic fell back in his seat as though someone had pushed him. "Meggie? What would you be wanting with her?"

Cavan reached into the inner breast pocket of his sport coat and removed some papers that he slid across the desk. "You'll recognize this as the marriage contract between your granddaughter and Sean Farrell. I won it from Hugh Farrell in a card game a few nights ago. Everything is quite legal."

Padraic read it through, including a newly added paragraph transferring the contract to Cavan. "I don't understand what you want me to do with this," he finally said when he'd finished reading. "Am I supposed to buy you out?"

"Not at all," Cavan said evenly. "You're supposed to give the bride away."

"You can't be serious! This—" he waved the paper in the air "—was a contract between friendly families. If you think I'm going to let Meggie marry some ex-convict..."

Cavan's blue eyes turned to steel. "Let's get something straight, O'Neill. I spent five years in an Irish prison for something I didn't do, and no one except Hugh Farrell knows that better than you. My only crime was that of a stablehand daring to run off with your precious granddaughter."

"You would have ruined Caroline's life!"

A corner of Cavan's mouth lifted cynically, saying more than words could about what had been done to his own life. Cavan handed him one more sheet of paper. Padraic O'Neill picked it up, but stared at Cavan over the top of it for a long moment before finally lowering his eyes to read the print that said that he had conspired with Hugh Farrell to wrongfully imprison Cavan Gallagher. Hugh's signature was scrawled at the bottom. "You expect me to sign this?" he asked, tossing it onto his desk.

"That's right."

He rose from behind his desk and paced the length of the room while Cavan rose as well and leaned casually against the edge of the desk to watch. Finally, Padraic stopped in front of him. "If I sign, you leave Meggie alone."

Cavan shook his head. "No. I'm still going to marry her."

"Then I won't sign."

Cavan picked up the paper and looked down at it. "It's your choice, O'Neill. As I said, I intend to marry her whether you sign this or not. The difference is that if you sign, Meggie will never find out about what you did. At least not from me."

"And if I don't sign?"

"I think you know the answer to that."

The old man's eyes narrowed. "What are you threatening me with?"

"I never threaten. What I'm telling you is that if she doesn't agree to marry me, then I'll tell her what her grandfather did all those years ago to an innocent man. What do you suppose her reaction will be?"

"She'll never believe you."

"How sure are you?" Cavan asked in a deadly quiet voice that held no conscience at all about what he was doing.

The old man wiped some perspiration from his forehead. "Why do you want to hurt Meggie? She had nothing to do with any of this. She was away at school ten years ago when all of this was happening. She doesn't even know about you and Caroline."

"I don't particularly want to hurt her, but if I need to do it in order to get to you, then I will, with no apologies. Meghan is my revenge."

Padraic snatched the paper from Cavan's hand, and without reading it again, roughly signed his name to it and threw the pen sharply to the desk.

Cavan picked up the paper, folded it and slipped it into his jacket pocket.

Padraic was grasping at straws. "I'll pay you to leave Meggie alone. I'll give you enough money to live on for the rest of your life."

"Oh, you'll pay me all right, but through your business, not your guilt money."

Padraic had turned away from Cavan, but at the younger man's words, he turned to face him. "You are the man behind AmeriTextiles, aren't you?" he asked, already knowing the answer.

"That's right."

Padraic reached out a less than steady hand to pull on a tapestried bell cord.

The same maid who had let Cavan in opened the doors. "Yes, sir?"

"Where is my granddaughter?"

"She's in the stables."

"Tell her she's needed in the library right away."

"Yes, sir."

A tense silence filled the room again as they both waited. When Meggie finally arrived ten minutes later, her face was streaked with dirt, and her heavy hair, which had been pulled into a ponytail, straggled around her face. She smiled a greeting at her grandfather, but her smile faded at the sight of the man with him. "Cavan?"

He rose and looked at her, but it was as though he didn't really see her. "Meghan."

Meggie's eyes remained on him, devouring him, afraid that if she blinked he would be gone. He looked much as he had all those years ago, but older. The grooves in his cheeks were deeper and there was a network of lines around the outer corners of his still remarkably blue eyes. His skin was tanned, his hair a little too long, which on him looked wonderful.

"Meggie?"

She started at her grandfather's voice and really looked at him for the first time since entering the library. He was several shades redder than the brisk Irish air could account for. Wordlessly he pushed some papers across his desk toward her and Meggie picked them up, reading them once quickly, and then more slowly.

Then she raised her eyes to Cavan. "I don't understand," she said quietly. "This is the marriage contract my father worked out with the Farrell family."

"That's right. The contract now belongs to me."

"How?"

"I won it in a poker game with Hugh Farrell."

To Cavan's surprise, Meggie's eyes twinkled with amusement. "You can't be serious."

Cavan said nothing, but he certainly didn't look as though he were playing a game.

Meggie looked from Cavan to her grandfather and back to Cavan again. The anger in the room was palpable, and Meggie grew more serious. "Do you want to marry me?" she asked Cavan.

"I expect you to fulfill the terms of the contract."

"I don't suppose you could put it in somewhat more romantic terms, could you?" she asked dryly.

"There's nothing romantic about any of this, Meghan."

His attitude toward her was disconcertingly impersonal. It was as though there were a heavy curtain between them cutting off communication. The main focus of his attention was her grandfather. "When would you like my answer?"

"Now."

Meggie looked down at the contract and sighed. "This isn't the way I thought it would be."

"What isn't?"

"Your asking me to marry you." It was obvious to Meggie that whatever attraction had occurred on that long-ago afternoon had been one-sided. So what was he after? Her money? Meggie walked to the window and stared blindly outside for a long time, then suddenly she turned to her grandfather. "Would you mind leaving us alone for a minute?"

He looked from his granddaughter to Cavan, his jaw tightening. Without a word, he strode from the room, anger in every line of his still lean frame.

When the doors had closed behind him, Meggie moved toward Cavan and stood in front of him until he lowered his eyes to her. And again she had the feeling that he was looking through rather than at her. "Why are you doing this? Why do you want to marry me?"

"I have my reasons."

"Which you don't intend to share with me."

He said nothing.

She walked slowly across the long room, searching for some kind of reasonable explanation; remembering the conversation between them long ago. "Are you using this marriage as a way of getting back at the Farrells?"

"Why do you say that?"

"They need my money. It's common knowledge in the village. If you marry me, Sean Farrell can't, and if he can't marry me, his family can't get at my money."

"You have it all worked out, don't you, Meggie?"

"Revenge. What an awful reason for marriage," she said softly, her back still to him. "What if I say no?"

"You won't."

Meggie turned away from the window. "And what makes you so sure?"

"It's a legal contract. Perhaps the Farrells wouldn't have given your grandfather a hard time if you hadn't lived up to it, but I will."

"You mean you'd take us to court?"

"That's right. And I'd probably win a large financial settlement. That's something I think you probably realize your grandfather can ill afford at the moment."

"You would ruin my grandfather simply to get back at Hugh Farrell?"

Cavan said nothing.

"All right," Meggie said after a moment. "I'll marry you." But her reasons had nothing to do with her grandfather. She didn't for a moment believe that a court of law would force a woman to marry against her will, or punish her family because she made a free choice. Though Irish courts could be strange at times....

She hated to start out this way with him though.

"I'll be in touch about the arrangements," he said coolly as he headed for the door. "I can find my way out."

As soon as Cavan had gone, her grandfather came in. "What happened?"

"I'm going to marry him."

Part of the man was relieved that she wouldn't be finding out about what had happened all those years ago, and part of him was filled with a terrible sadness. "You don't have to, you know."

Meggie turned back to the window and watched Cavan as he folded his long frame into his low, black sports car. "Grandfather," she said quietly, "do you remember what we were talking about in the cemetery the other night?''

His heart constricted as he stared at the back of her head. There was a long pause before he could answer her without his voice wavering. "Are you saying that Cavan Gallagher is the man you're in love with?"

Meggie turned her head and met her grandfather's look with a direct one of her own. "Since the first and only time I met him."

He tiredly rubbed his forehead and let out a long, heartfelt sigh. "Meggie, Meggie. Why can't you ever do things the easy way?"

A smile touched her eyes. "It's not my nature."

"You're making a terrible mistake. The man cares nothing for you. He doesn't care anything for anyone because he's so filled with anger and hatred."

"He has a right to be. But I think you're wrong about his not caring anything for me. More than anger at Hugh Farrell drove him back here. I think maybe he fell in love with me the way I did with him, but he hasn't recognized it for what it is yet."

"He's not capable of love, Meggie."

Meggie walked over to her grandfather and kissed him on the cheek. "Circumstances have made him the way he is, and circumstances can unmake him. You'll see." She started for the door, but her grandfather's voice stopped her.

"Meggie?"

"Umm?"

"There are things you don't know."

She looked at him inquiringly with her lovely hazel eyes.

He opened his mouth to speak, but closed it over the words. He couldn't tell her. She'd never forgive him.

"Grandfather?"

He shook his head. "Never mind. I'll see you at dinner."

"Not tonight. I'm going to my cottage in the north for a few days. I need to think."

"What about your job?"

"School is closed, remember? The teacher is free for a week. I'll see you when I get back."

When she'd gone, he sank into the chair behind his desk, looking suddenly older.

Chapter Three

A few days later Meggie parked her car in front of the Farrell manor. Grabbing an armload of books and notepads from her passenger seat, she made her way up the wide stone staircase to the front door and jabbed at the incongruously modern doorbell button with her elbow. The housekeeper opened the door and stood there with her hands on her generous hips. "Well, Meggie O'Neill, what are you doing here?"

"Hi, Millie. Would you please tell Sean I'm here with the books I told him about? He's going to help me with some Gaelic-to-English translations for the language class I'm teaching."

Millie frowned at her in surprise, then took some of the books out of Meggie's overloaded arms and carried them inside for her. "Hasn't he called you?"

"He couldn't have even if he'd wanted to. Nobody could have. I've been at my cottage near the North Sea. There's no phone."

Millie set the books on an antique table in the salon and Meggie followed suit, then shook her arms a little to get the circulation going again. "That would explain it. Sean left with his parents."

Meggie still wasn't getting it. "On a vacation?"

The housekeeper frowned even more. "No, Meggie. A man named Cavan Gallagher won the house and the land from Hugh Farrell in a card game. The Farrells have moved out."

Meggie's lips parted softly in amazement as she dropped onto the couch behind her. "So he has everything of theirs, then."

"Everything."

"Has Cavan moved in yet?"

"Yesterday."

"And you're staying on with him?"

"I'm staying with the house." Millie was very possessive about the home she'd worked in for twenty-five years.

"Millie, I won't be home for dinner tonight." Cavan's voice came from behind Meggie, who jumped to her feet, her heart pounding.

"Yes, sir," the housekeeper said crisply and then left the room.

As he waved Meggie back to the couch and took a chair across from her, her eyes wandered over him. She liked the way he always looked as though he just threw his clothes on and they happened to suit him perfectly. At the moment he had on pleated tan trousers and an oversized white shirt with the sleeves casually rolled halfway up his forearms. "I've arranged for the marriage ceremony to be held here in two days."

"Two days?" To say she was surprised was to put it mildly.

"I'll send someone to help you move your things whenever you're ready."

"Wait a minute! I'm still working on the two days. I can't possibly be ready that quickly. It doesn't give me enough time."

"Time for what?"

She couldn't believe he even had to ask the question. "For sending invitations and planning a reception. My sister is off heaven knows where. I'll never be able to get in touch with her in time. I don't even have a dress to wear."

"Meghan," he said quietly, "we aren't having a wedding; we're having a marriage ceremony. And we aren't having a reception afterward because there's nothing to celebrate."

His words slapped her back to reality. For the past several days as she sat alone on the cliffs overlooking the North Sea she'd done a lot of thinking. Hard thinking. She wanted to marry Cavan. She had to, otherwise he'd walk out of her life without ever realizing that he was in love with her, too. Her eyes searched his face, looking for some sign of what he was feeling and finding none. "You don't believe in pulling your punches, do you?"

He said nothing.

"Look, Cavan, I'm not deluding myself about the reason for our marriage, but you have to understand that I'm a real person with real feelings, and I expect to be treated with consideration. Telling me that we're going to be married in two days is inconsiderate, to say the least."

Cavan found himself looking at Meggie, really looking at her, for the first time since he'd returned to Ireland. What he saw was a lovely woman with intelligent eyes who had an appealing dignity. Something stirred in him, but then was gone as quickly as it had come. "I apologize."

Meggie looked at him in surprise. Those were two words she never expected to hear cross his lips. "Thank you."

"I still, though, see no reason to either delay the marriage or make a production of it."

Meggie knew when it was futile to argue. "All right," she reluctantly agreed. "May my family come?"

Cavan said nothing.

"Or I should say my grandfather. I haven't been able to reach my sister. Her husband died just over a year ago and since then she's done a lot of traveling."

"I definitely want your grandfather there."

Meggie studied Cavan for a long moment. "You don't like him, do you?"

Cavan got to his feet without answering. "I have an appointment."

Meggie rose as well, feeling dismissed. "I better take my books."

"You might as well leave them," he said as he walked her to the door and opened it. "You'll just have to bring them back."

Meggie walked through the door and started to turn to say something else, but the door closed behind her. She stood there for a full thirty seconds, and even raised her hand to knock, but it fell back to her side. With a sigh, she walked slowly down the steps to her car.

Nobody said it would be easy. But she never dreamed he'd be so hard to reach. Cavan's emotions were buried so deeply she wondered if she'd ever get through to them.

On the short drive to her house, she pushed thoughts of Cavan from her mind. She had to or her courage to go through with the wedding would have failed her. Marriage wasn't a frivolous thing in Ireland. It was looked upon as permanent. If she was making a mistake, it was something that would follow her for the rest of her life, not just the few months it would take to get a divorce.

After parking the car, she went into the house and ran up the stairs to her room to start searching for an appropriate wedding dress. Time and again she pulled dresses off the racks and held them against her, but nothing was right, and she finally realized what the problem was. She wanted to look like a bride, because no matter how Cavan viewed this wedding, it meant something to her. Maybe she couldn't invite her friends, and maybe there wouldn't be a reception to celebrate, but he couldn't stop her from looking like a bride, and that's exactly what she intended to do.

With renewed determination, she grabbed her purse and ran down the stairs to her car. She drove quickly over the narrow winding roads to the main street of the village and parked in front of a small shop. With her fingers mentally crossed, she walked in and stood for a moment as her eyes wandered over the dozens of bolts of cloth that filled long tables.

"Meggie!"

Meggie turned with a smile toward the owner of the shop. "Hello, Bridgit."

"What can I do for you today?"

She fingered a soft wool tartan. "I need some material for a wedding dress."

Bridgit's eyes widened in surprise. "I hadn't heard that you and Sean had set a date."

"I'm not marrying Sean."

"But, I thought . . ."

"I'm marrying a man by the name of Cavan Gallagher in two days, so I have to get started on the dress right away."

"Two days! But you can't make a wedding dress in two days."

"I can if I use a simple dress pattern and enlarge upon it."

"You do tend toward full skirts," Bridgit said thoughtfully. "Did you have a particular pattern in mind?"

"It's a dress I made last year, Bridgit, with a full white skirt, V-necked bodice, long sleeves, navy-blue piping to give it something of a nautical look. You helped me with the pattern."

"Of course." She pictured the dress in her mind's eye. "And I can see the possibilities. Take away the piping, add length and even more fullness to the skirt, wider sleeves... it'll certainly be different from most wedding gowns, but lovely. What kind of material?"

Meggie smiled a half smile. "There's the rub. I was hoping for white satin. Do you have any?"

Now it was Bridgit's turn to smile. "I thought no one was ever going to ask me that question again. Follow me."

Bridgit led her into a storage room, and way back on a table, wrapped in plastic, were yards and yards of white satin. "To make a long story short, last year I was supposed to make a wedding dress for someone, but the wedding was called off, and I got stuck with a lot of material. Consider it yours for half price."

Meggie fingered the rich material. "Oh, Bridgit, I could kiss you."

"Can I help you with the making of the dress?"

A soft smile touched Meggie's eyes, telling Bridgit more than words ever could have about Meggie's feelings for the man she was going to marry. "No, thank you. This is one I'd like to do on my own."

"All right, but if you run into problems, don't hesitate to call." She lifted the heavy bolt of material from the table and put it in Meggie's arms. "I'll put this on your bill. And don't forget to let me know how it turns out."

Meggie raced the material home and upstairs into the sewing room. And that was where her grandfather found her hours later, sitting in the middle of the floor, surrounded by yards of white satin. He sat in a chair near her and watched as she painstakingly cut the material.

"Wedding dress?" he asked tonelessly.

"I hope so."

Silence filled the room for a moment, but Meggie felt her grandfather's thoughts, and knew what he was going to say even before he spoke a word. "You don't have to go through with this, Meggie."

"Yes, I do."

"You have no idea what you're getting into. You know next to nothing about the man—but what little you do know should give you pause."

"I love him, grandfather."

"He doesn't love you."

"But I think he does. And if he doesn't now, he will eventually."

"And if he never falls in love with you. What then?"

Meggie's scissors paused for a moment, then began slicing through the material again. "I'll worry about that when the time comes."

"It'll be too late then, child."

She put the scissors on the floor next to her and gave her grandfather her full attention. "I don't want to talk about this anymore. I'm twenty-three years old, and if marrying Cavan Gallagher is a mistake, then it's my mistake to make. Regardless of how much I love and respect you, you're not going to change my mind about this."

She went back to work and her grandfather stared at the top of her head feeling more helpless than he ever had before. All of her life, Meggie had been optimistic. Always looking for the bright side. Always a dreamer. And the dreamers of this world often got hurt when cold, hard reality interrupted.

Little did Cavan know just how deeply this act of revenge cut. It had been so important to the family all those years ago that Caroline not marry Cavan. Now Cavan was taking Meggie away from him and there was nothing he could do to stop him. No matter what he did, Padraic knew he'd alienate Meggie, and he couldn't bear that. This granddaughter meant everything to him.

Without saying anything else, he rose from the chair and left the room.

Meggie's gaze followed him out. She hated hurting him, but this was one time when she had to follow her heart or spend the rest of her life wondering "what if?"

Two days later, Cavan stood in the open French doors, his shoulder leaning against the frame, and stared outside. Mist rolled gently over the craggy land. All that time in prison, and then all those years traveling the world, gambling to make money and then investing the money he won, the thing he'd missed the most was the soft Irish weather. Strange how he hadn't known that until now.

He glanced at his watch. In just one hour he would be married to Meghan O'Neill and the revenge he'd planned for nearly ten years would be complete. He was really looking forward to seeing her grandfather's face while the vows were being exchanged. This had nothing to do with Meggie's sister anymore. Cavan had long since put Caroline out of his mind. He could barely remember what she looked like. Padraic O'Neill had helped to take away five years of his life, and now Cavan would be taking something equally as dear to Padraic.

A smile slowly curved his mouth at the thought. Revenge was indeed sweet.

"Mr. Gallagher?"

He turned to find his hefty, no-nonsense house-keeper standing just behind him.

"I think it's time to dress. The priest will be here in a few minutes."

Cavan looked down at the unstructured jacket he was wearing over a sweater. "I am dressed."

"But not for a wedding. I've taken the liberty of laying out your tuxedo."

"Millie," he said with one of his rare smiles, "you're a pushy woman."

"That I am, sir, and if you don't like it, feel free to fire me. But if you intend to keep me on—and I personally think you should unless you want the place to fall down around your ears—then I'd appreciate your doing as I tell you, at least about this matter."

"No wonder the Farrells left you here when they moved."

"So, you'll wear it?"

"No. But I have a few things to do before the ceremony." He walked past her toward the stairs and paused. "Oh," he turned back to her, "did you put Miss O'Neill's things in the guest bedroom?"

"I did—but are you sure that's where you want them?"

"I'm sure."

Her serious eyes followed Cavan out of the room. She didn't understand what was going on here. The man couldn't have been more at ease if it had been a perfect stranger getting married rather than himself. And to put his new bride in the guest room? Who had ever heard of such a thing?

The doorbell rang and Millie hurried to answer it. Meggie stood there, a shy smile touching her mouth. "Hello, Millie. Do you think anyone will mind if I dress here?"

"I don't, and I'm the one you're talking to. Come in, come in." She stepped aside and waved Meggie into the house. "Is that your dress?" she asked, nodding at the bundle in Meggie's arms.

"I just finished it."

"Well, don't just stand there. Let me see it."

Meggie had known Millie all of her life and was used to her gruffness. She dropped the dress to its full length and lifted the plastic bag covering it.

"Oh, Meggie," she whispered, "it's beautiful. If only I could have talked that husband-to-be of yours into changing into a tuxedo. He's going to feel a little foolish standing next to you."

Meggie smiled wryly. "Somehow I doubt that. He probably won't even notice what I'm wearing."

"Then he's a blind man."

Meggie smiled fondly at the housekeeper. "Thank you. I needed that. Where would you like me to change?"

"The blue guest room." She started to take Meggie upstairs, but the doorbell rang again. "Oh, dear. You know where it is, don't you?"

"As well as in my own home."

"Which is what this place will be to you shortly." She kissed Meggie on the cheek. "If you need any help, give a call." Then she hurried off.

Meggie climbed the rest of the stairs and walked down the long hall, pausing for just a moment in front of the door to the master bedroom, wondering if Cavan was in there. She wanted to see him so badly to reassure herself that everything would work out. She even lifted her hand to knock, but it fell back to her side. What kind of guarantees could he give her?

With a sigh, she started down the hall again and turned into the guest room.

About forty minutes later there was a knock on her door. "It's time, Meggie," came Millie's voice. "Everyone's here. Are you ready?"

"What do you mean by everyone?"

"You'll see when you come down."

Meggie looked critically into the mirror and decided she liked what she saw. The white satin dress was perfect in the way it fit her upper body and flowed like a ball gown from her slender waist. She had braided her long hair into a single plait that she'd wound around her head and then set a circle of flowers over. It was a simple style that suited her.

"I'll see you downstairs in a minute," she called back to the housekeeper.

"Don't be much longer than that. Everyone's waiting."

Meggie heard her walk away. Suddenly she sank onto the edge of the bed with her hand over her thudding heart. What on earth was she doing? This was for the rest of her life. What if she was making a mistake? What if she was wrong about Cavan?

She took a deep breath and slowly exhaled, then rose. With great concentration, she smoothed a wrinkle from the front of her dress, then with a last look in the mirror, she made her way downstairs to the drawing room where she stood unnoticed in the doorway for several seconds, watching in amazement.

Father Flaherty, his half glasses low on his nose, was speaking in quiet tones with her grandfather. Millie was there with a nun from the orphanage where Meggie taught, standing in the middle of fifteen chattering children. One of the little boys broke away from the crowd and tried to run past Meggie with another little boy hot on his heels. Meggie hunkered down and laughingly caught one in each arm and hugged them. "What a nice surprise! What are all of you doing here?"

"Father Flaherty brought us."

"He said there'd be lots of cake and stuff."

"Oh, dear," she looked over at Millie with distressed eyes. "I don't think . . ."

Millie walked over and took the little boys' hands in hers and led them to some chairs. "You bet there is. More than you'll ever be able to eat."

Meggie started to rise, but stayed where she was when she saw a little girl walking toward her, sucking her thumb, a doll clutched in a thin arm. She leaned against Meggie, and Meggie wrapped a warm arm around her. "Hello, Sarah. I'm glad you could come."

Sarah was only three. She had come to the orphanage six months earlier when her parents were killed in an explosion in Londonderry. Meggie loved all of the children she worked with, but there was something about Sarah, with her mass of brown curls and big blue eyes, that had caught at Meggie's heart the first time she'd seen her. She rose, with Sarah in her arms, and stood talking softly to her, unaware of the eyes of the man she was about to marry watching her. Unaware of the narrowed gaze of the attractive woman standing beside Cavan, watching him watch Meggie.

Meggie carried the child over to Father Flaherty and put her in his arms, then kissed him on the cheek. "Thank you."

"You're welcome. Are you about ready?"

Meggie glanced around the room and found Cavan. Their eyes met and held for a long moment. "Yes, I guess so."

Her grandfather hugged her tightly against him. "I wish all the best for you, Meggie. You know that."

"I know."

"It's not too late to change your mind." He sounded almost hopeful.

Meggie pulled slightly away and smiled at him. "I know, but I won't."

"Then I'll say no more about it."

"Thank you." She kissed him, and turned to find Cavan standing next to her.

Meggie's heartbeat accelerated, the way she imagined it always would when he was near. Meggie swallowed hard and concentrated on keeping her breathing calm and even.

"Are you ready?" he asked.

"I think so. And you?" It was impossible to read his eyes.

"I have some papers for you to sign first."

"What kind of papers?"

Cavan took her arm and led her to the attractive woman he'd been standing with earlier. "Meghan O'Neill, this is my attorney, Jessica Pierson."

Meggie politely extended her hand. "How do you do?"

The other woman looked at Meggie's hand for a still moment before taking it in hers.

"Jessica has prepared some documents that say, in effect, that what is yours is yours and what is mine is mine, and if this marriage ends in divorce we walk away with what we each brought into it."

"That's fair."

"And your grandfather has already given me your dowry. I don't wish to accept it, so the second paper I need you to sign is simply one turning that dowry over to you for your own use."

Meggie took an offered pen from his attorney's fingers and signed the papers. "Anything else?"

"That's all." Then he spoke with the attorney. "File these away, Jessica." Then he took a single, folded sheet of paper from his inner jacket pocket. "And you know what to do with this one. There's no need for you to stay for the wedding. I'll see you in the States shortly."

She shouldered her smart leather briefcase, her eyes on Cavan. "I wish you'd reconsider this marriage. It isn't necessary. The other things you've done more than compensate—"

"Goodbye, Jessica," Cavan cut her off.

Meggie watched the exchange with interested eyes as Jessica turned on her heel and left the room. "She's in love with you," she told Cavan quietly.

He glanced down at Meggie and then looked away. "What she is or isn't is none of your business."

One of the children tugged at Meggie's hand and she moved slightly away from Cavan as she bent to speak with her. His eyes moved over her lovely, strong body with its soft curves encased in white satin, the skirt billowing out around her, and he felt something unfamiliar stir within him. The woman who was going to be his wife radiated a friendly warmth and energy that had filled the room the moment she entered. He had never met anyone like that before, and he found it intriguing—and just a little disconcerting.

Suddenly he stepped forward and took her arm. "Let's get this over with."

She walked with him to the priest, who took her gently into his arms and kissed her cheek. "What a beautiful bride you are, Meggie...isn't she, Paddy?"

Her grandfather's eyes softened as they rested on her. "That she is."

The sun was setting and the room was growing dark so Millie turned on some lamps to lend a friendly glow and got the children seated.

Cavan moved next to Meggie, so close that his strong arm brushed against her, sending a shiver of awareness coursing through her body. Father Flaherty stood before them and cleared his throat. "At the request of Mr. Gallagher, I'll keep the ceremony simple."

And he did. After a few remarks about love and commitment, and the meaning of marriage, he recited the vows. Cavan repeated his first, in a monotone, devoid of any emotion; any feeling. That was when it really hit Meggie. All of the "what ifs" she'd refused to think about since accepting the marriage contract now flooded through her mind. What if Cavan never fell in love with her?

Meggie's throat constricted, and when it was her turn to say the words, there was a noticeable hesitation before she was able to. Cavan looked down at her, and what he saw gave him pause. She was obviously waging an inner battle. Until now she'd behaved as though this were all a game, but he realized as he studied her pale profile that this was anything but a game to her.

Suddenly, as though she'd made a decision, she straightened her shoulders and raised her chin almost defiantly and repeated the vows in her low, melodic voice.

When Cavan took her hand in his to slip on the simple wedding band, he felt her tremble. He looked down at her unsteady hand and tightened his around it just a little to comfort her. Meggie looked at him gratefully and a gentle smile touched her mouth.

That smile, more than anything else, brought him an uncomfortable awareness of what he was doing to her. None of this was her fault. She might be an

O'Neill, but she was an innocent one caught in the middle of an ugly situation. An urge to protect her suddenly welled within Cavan. He had to stop the ceremony. His mouth opened to say the words—but then he saw Meggie's grandfather standing behind her, looking as grieved as though he'd lost Meggie forever. The reasons for this marriage rushed back to him and Meggie as a person faded into insignificance. He had a purpose in doing this, and he listened to the words pronouncing them husband and wife in stony silence.

Father Flaherty smiled at both of them a moment later. "You may now kiss the bride."

Meggie turned toward Cavan, sensing his reluctance. "Please, don't embarrass me," she asked softly in a voice only he could hear.

Cavan put his hands lightly on her shoulders and drew her toward him. Hazel eyes gazed into blue. As he lowered his mouth to hers, Meggie's lips parted with soft invitation. He only intended his mouth to brush hers, but Meggie moved a fraction closer, rising on her toes to meet him halfway. Their lips touched tentatively, for only a moment.

"You call that a kiss?" asked one of the older boys from the orphanage in disgust.

Meggie grinned at Cavan, and though he didn't smile back, he put his hand at Meggie's waist and pulled her closer, then firmly lowered his mouth to hers. It was a long, slow kiss that left Meggie aching for more. When he finally raised his head, he looked at the boy who had asked the question. "How was that?"

GALLAGHER'S LADY   53

The boy winked and gave the high sign.

Cavan shook his head. "Cheeky kid."

Meggie watched her husband. Husband, she thought, what a lovely word. She watched him with a half smile. Well, at least she'd discovered that somewhere inside him was a sense of humor.

What she couldn't see was his surprise at the depth of his own reaction to kissing her. Being attracted to Meghan O'Neill wasn't something he'd expected. When he looked back at Meggie as the children moved forward to congratulate them, she moved closer.

"You've got your revenge," she said quietly. "Now what are you going to do with me?"

He had no answer. For the first time Cavan realized that his planning had only taken him to this moment, but not beyond. What *was* he going to do with her?

Meggie could tell that her words had struck a nerve and a dimple creased her cheek. Cavan Gallagher had a dilemma and she was it. The children were tugging at her, and as she bent to hug the smaller children, Cavan's eyes clashed over her head with those of Padraic O'Neill.

Until Father Flaherty stepped between them. "I wish you both the best," he said, shaking Cavan's hand and hugging Meggie when she'd finished with the children. Then he looked at her grandfather who was speaking with Millie. "I'm afraid you're going to have to work on Paddy, though. He seems less than pleased about this."

Meggie was a little surprised that her grandfather hadn't confided in Father Flaherty about the contract. "He'll come around."

"He can be mighty stubborn at times."

"I won't give up," she smiled.

"I'll work on him, too. But right now I'd better lead these children to the food or there'll be no living with them."

As soon as the priest had gone, her grandfather walked over to them. "I'm going to be leaving now, Meggie."

"You don't have to, you know."

"I do, Meggie. I can't watch this any longer." He completely ignored Cavan. "Call me if you need me."

She followed him a short distance away from Cavan and caught his arm. "Grandfather, Cavan isn't a bad man."

"How would you know what kind of man he is?"

Meggie's eyes met Cavan's across the room. "My instincts about people rarely let me down."

Her grandfather's jaw grew taut. "Your instincts aren't as good as you think, Meggie," he said quietly as he walked away from her.

She didn't have time to think about what he said because a small hand tugged at her dress and Meggie looked down to find Sarah there, smiling up at her.

Meggie stooped and picked her up. "Hello, sweetheart."

"'Lo."

"Why aren't you eating cake with the others?"

"I'm tired."

Cavan walked over to them. "I have some calls to make. I'll be in the library."

"Can't you wait until the children go?"

"I told you I didn't want anyone here." He didn't sound angry. Just matter-of-fact.

Suddenly Sarah reached out and wrapped her arms around Cavan's neck. He had no choice but to hold her as Meggie let go, and the little girl rested her head on Cavan's shoulder, a doll dangling from one of her hands.

He looked helplessly at Meggie, who just smiled at him. "If that doesn't humanize you a little, nothing will." Then she waved her fingers at him as she headed from the room. "I'm going to check on the others."

Millie had set up a table just for the children with lovely cakes and pastries, and they were thoroughly enjoying themselves. She found Millie looking stern as she admonished a boy whose mouth was so full he couldn't possibly fit another crumb into it. Meggie hugged her. "You should have told me what you were doing. I could have helped with some of the baking."

"I thought it best that you be able to say with complete honesty that you didn't know anything about it."

"I think you had that exactly right. Thank you." She looked around the buzzing room. "This is wonderful."

Father Flaherty clapped his hands and everyone grew suddenly quiet. "All right, children. Say thank-you and get your things together. It's time to go home."

Groans went up around the room, but they did as they were told.

Meggie walked over to the priest and looped her arm through his. "We'll wrap up what's left and send it to the orphanage."

He absently patted her hand. "Where's Sarah?"

"I'll get her." Meggie went into the salon where the ceremony had taken place, but it was empty, so she opened the door to the library and looked in. Cavan was behind the desk, true to his word, talking on the telephone. Sarah was sound asleep on the couch clutching her doll with Cavan's sport coat as her blanket. "They're going now," Meggie explained as she gently lifted Sarah.

Cavan inclined his head and continued his conversation.

Meggie went back to where the children were and handed Sarah to Father Flaherty. "Try not to wake her."

The other children were all climbing into two vans that were waiting outside. Father Flaherty handed Sarah to one of the older children to hold so that he could drive, and the nun got behind the wheel of the other van.

Meggie and the housekeeper stood in the doorway and waved them off, then closed the door against the brisk night air. Meggie stood there for a moment and listened. "It's so quiet."

"It is that." Millie began clearing away the food and Meggie started to help, but the housekeeper lightly slapped the top of her hand. "Stop that this instant. You'll get something on your lovely dress."

Meggie looked down at herself with a half smile. "Do you suppose anyone would notice?"

"More than you might think." She balanced several plates and headed for the kitchen. "Dinner will be ready soon, and I'll be out of here shortly thereafter."

"Where are you going?"

"I thought I'd spend the night at my sister's house."

"You don't have to do that."

Millie just smiled and went into the kitchen.

Meggie strolled through the house. It was rather strange to think that she was going to be living in this house she'd spent so much time in as a child. When she got to the library, she knocked and walked in. Cavan was still on the phone. She sat on the couch where Sarah had been and watched him. His black hair was still a bit too long in back. She loved the contrast of his dark hair and skin and blue eyes. He rose from his chair and walked to the window, still talking on the phone, and stood staring out with his back to her. Meggie allowed her eyes the freedom to roam over his broad shoulders and down his length to his nice rear end and strong, long legs. Her husband was a very, very attractive man.

Cavan finally finished his phone conversation. He walked back to his desk, hung up the phone and stood looking at Meggie. "Is everyone gone?"

"Except for Millie. She's getting dinner ready."

"I could use a drink. How about you?"

"Dry sherry would be nice, thank you."

She watched as he poured hers at a bar at one end of the room, and then fixed himself a stiff Irish whiskey. When he handed her the sherry, he lifted his glass very slightly in a silent toast and drank it down. Meggie took a ladylike sip, her eyes never leaving him over the rim of her glass.

"What kind of business are you in?"

"Various."

A long silence fell between them.

"Whatever will we talk about in fifty years?" Meggie finally asked in a voice tinged with amusement.

A corner of Cavan's mouth lifted.

"Dinner is ready." Millie's voice cut through the silence.

Cavan signaled to Meggie that she should walk ahead of him. The satin swished as only satin could as she moved through the house to the dining room. Millie had tried her best to make the vast table cozy by seating them across from each other at one end with a low flower arrangement and candles between.

Cavan's hands accidentally brushed Meggie's arms as he pushed her chair in, sending a delicious shiver winding through her. How was it, she wondered, that in all of her twenty-three years and all of the attractive men she'd dated, none of them ever began to make her tingle the way this man could with just a casual touch?

She smiled at him when he sat across from her, but Cavan didn't smile back and hers faded slightly. Millie served them the first course, chattering all the while. When she left, the silence that hung in the room was oppressive. "How do you like the house?" Meggie asked conversationally before taking a sip of soup.

"It's a house."

"I've always found it to be a little dark. Would you mind if I added some brighter colors?"

"You can do what you want." He sounded completely uninterested.

"I promise not to spend too much money."

"Spend as much as you care to. It doesn't matter."

Meggie didn't have much of an appetite. She set her spoon on the plate next to the bowl. "Are you planning on doing anything with the horses here? I understand there's some good breeding stock, though the Farrells never cared to go into that aspect of raising horses."

"What I decide to do or not to do with the horses is my business."

Meggie grew quiet and toyed with the napkin on her lap.

Cavan looked at her downcast eyes and felt a pang of guilt.

Both of them were quiet as Millie removed their bowls and served the second course. When she'd gone, Cavan sat there for several seconds, moving the food around on his plate absently with his fork until he finally gave up in disgust and left the table to stare out the window. In all those years of plotting his revenge, the imagined ending was always the same. He triumphed over Hugh Farrell and Padraic O'Neill and was himself purged of all anger, ready to get on with his life. But it wasn't working out that way. He was still angry, and he was beginning to wonder if that was the only emotion he was capable of feeling anymore.

He gazed at Meggie's reflection in the window as she sat quietly at the table staring at his back. He'd never met anyone like her before, and he didn't quite know what to do with her. He had dragged her right into the center of things, and now that she was there, he had no use for her. No use whatsoever.

"I'm going for a walk," he said suddenly as he walked from the room. "I don't know what time I'll be back."

When he had gone, Meggie gave up all pretense of eating and rose from the table. How was she ever going to make him see the light if he wouldn't even talk to her?

When Millie came in to clear away the dishes, she looked curiously at Meggie. "Where is he?"

"My—husband—went for a walk. I think I'll go to bed."

Millie clicked her tongue in disapproval. "What kind of way is that to start a honeymoon?"

"No way at all," Meggie said with a sigh. "Thank you for the nice dinner. I'm sorry I couldn't eat more."

"My sister's cats will be grateful."

Meggie headed up the stairs, but stopped halfway up and leaned heavily against the banister, suddenly tired beyond words both emotionally and physically. It had been a long day.

Concentrating on putting one foot in front of the other, Meggie finished climbing the stairs and went to the guest room. Her things hung neatly in the armoire. She slipped out of her wedding dress and hung it away with a last affectionate look, and pulled out an old-fashioned nightgown that was one of her favorites. It was full, with yards of white material and feminine touches of lace. Then she removed the flowers from her hair, unbraided it and brushed it out in long, slow strokes.

When she was finished, she looked around the room. This was where he wanted her, obviously. But that didn't mean this was where she was going to sleep.

What Meggie did next was very difficult for her, but she left her room and walked down the hall to the master bedroom. She knocked softly on the door and listened, but there was no answer. Slowly she pushed the door open and, leaving the room in darkness, walked to the empty bed and climbed beneath the covers.

With a tired sigh, she relaxed against the pillows to wait. And wait. And wait. Once she thought she heard him on the stairs and her heart raced beneath her breast.

But he didn't come. Her heart slowed to normal and a terrible loneliness settled over Meggie. A wedding night to remember. Finally she drifted into an exhausted sleep.

Cavan came in from his walk and headed for the bar. He drank one whiskey and then another, and then tiredly rubbed his forehead.

When he climbed the stairs to his room, he didn't even turn on the light, but undressed in the dark and sank onto the bed. He lay there for a long time, his eyes open, staring at the ceiling.

Something moved next to him, and he raised up on an elbow, straining his eyes in the darkness to see, though he knew already who it was. A cloud moved from in front of the moon and there was Meggie, sleeping softly. Her auburn hair was spread out hap-hazardly over the pillow as though her sleep was a restless one. Still raised on an elbow, Cavan relaxed a little and rested his cheek on the palm of his hand as he studied the face of the woman he had married. The moonlight revealed her face in all of its delicate beauty. Cavan reached out a tentative hand and trailed the back of it down her smooth cheek. Meggie moved nearer to him, unconsciously snuggling against his body. Cavan started to get up to move to another room, but didn't. Instead, he lay back against his pillows while Meggie burrowed closer still. He put his arm gently around her shoulders—not knowing what else to do with it—and lay there listening to the quiet, even sounds of her breathing. Her cheek was against his bare chest, her hand lay lightly across his hard stomach.

He inhaled deeply the delicious scent of her hair and closed his eyes. Again some long-dead feelings stirred within him. Feelings he couldn't explain. It wasn't just sexual. He'd had his share of women over the years. But what he felt right now, with Meggie, was different.

He barely knew her, yet it somehow felt right to have her sleeping beside him.

Chapter Four

Meggie woke slowly the next morning, savoring the warm feeling of security that filled her. Cavan's shoulder moved slightly beneath her cheek and a contented smile curved her mouth—and then her eyes flew wide open. She sat up on her elbow and looked down at the sleeping man. He was on his back with his face turned away from her. A black shadow covered his cheeks. Meggie's gaze traveled over his strong throat to his smoothly muscled chest and down over his flat stomach, stopping out of necessity at his hips where a white sheet rode dangerously low.

Cavan stirred and turned his face toward her, and for the first time Meggie had the freedom to look her fill at the man she had married. The grooves in his cheeks weren't so noticeable in his sleep. His forehead was high and intelligent. His black eyebrows were straight slashes against his tanned skin. Her fingertip lightly touched his full, chiseled mouth and trailed down to the barely noticeable crease in his chin.

She felt rather than saw Cavan looking at her and raised her eyes to his. "Good morning."

He just looked at her. "What are you doing, Meghan?" he asked coolly.

She took her fingertip from his chin and moved slightly away from him. "Getting to know my husband."

He raised his hand and ran his fingers through his thick hair, his eyes still on her. "Next time ask your husband first."

Meggie's eyes dropped. "I'm sorry."

Cavan felt like a heel, but he couldn't reach out to Meggie to tell her that. Instead he got out of bed and walked into the adjoining bathroom. A moment later Meggie heard the shower running. She sat up, hugging her knees, and stared blindly at a picture hanging on the wall. A tear escaped from the corner of her eye. She was completely unaware of the man opening the bathroom door because he'd forgotten something, and standing there watching the tear's slow progress down her pale cheek. A muscle in Cavan's jaw worked as he lowered his head and quietly closed the door again.

Meggie sniffed once and brushed the tear away with the back of her hand. "If this is the way you are after only one day, Meggie O'Neill—Meggie Gallagher," she corrected herself aloud, "you've got problems. Now get it together, woman."

1. How do you rate _____
   (Please print book TITLE)

   1.6 ☐ excellent   .4 ☐ good   .2 ☐ not so good
   .5 ☐ very good   .3 ☐ fair   .1 ☐ poor

2. How likely are you to purchase another book:

   in this *series* ?   by this *author* ?
   2.1 ☐ definitely would purchase   3.1 ☐ definitely would purchase
   .2 ☐ probably would puchase   .2 ☐ probably would puchase
   .3 ☐ probably would not purchase   .3 ☐ probably would not purchase
   .4 ☐ definitely would not purchase   .4 ☐ definitely would not purchase

3. How does this book compare with similar books you usually read?

   4.1 ☐ far better than others   .2 ☐ better than others   .3 ☐ about the
   .4 ☐ not as good   .5 ☐ definitely not as good   same

4. Please check the statements you feel best describe this book.

   5. ☐ Easy to read   6. ☐ Too much violence/anger
   7. ☐ Realistic conflict   8. ☐ Wholesome/not too sexy
   9. ☐ Too sexy   10. ☐ Interesting characters
   11. ☐ Original plot   12. ☐ Especially romantic
   13. ☐ Not enough humor   14. ☐ Difficult to read
   15. ☐ Didn't like the subject   16. ☐ Good humor in story
   17. ☐ Too predictable   18. ☐ Not enough description of setting
   19. ☐ Believable characters   20. ☐ Fast paced
   21. ☐ Couldn't put the book down   22. ☐ Heroine too juvenile/weak/silly
   23. ☐ Made me feel good   24. ☐ Too many foreign/unfamiliar words
   25. ☐ Hero too dominating   26. ☐ Too wholesome/not sexy enough
   27. ☐ Not enough romance   28. ☐ Liked the setting
   29. ☐ Ideal hero   30. ☐ Heroine too independent
   31. ☐ Slow moving   32. ☐ Unrealistic conflict
   33. ☐ Not enough suspense   34. ☐ Sensuous/not too sexy
   35. ☐ Liked the subject   36. ☐ Too much description of setting

5. What *most* prompted you to buy this book?

   37. ☐ Read others in series   38. ☐ Title   39. ☐ Cover art
   40. ☐ Friend's recommendation   41. ☐ Author   42. ☐ In-store display
   43. ☐ TV, radio or magazine ad   44. ☐ Price   45. ☐ Story outline
   46. ☐ Ad inside other books   47. ☐ Other _____ (please specify)

6. Please indicate how many romance paperbacks you read in a month.

   48.1 ☐ 1 to 4   .2 ☐ 5 to 10   .3 ☐ 11 to 15   .4 ☐ more than 15

7. Please indicate your sex and age group.

   49.1 ☐ Male   50.1 ☐ under 15   .3 ☐ 25-34   .5 ☐ 50-64
   .2 ☐ Female   .2 ☐ 15-24   .4 ☐ 35-49   .6 ☐ 65 or older

8. Have you any additional comments about this book?

   _____ (51)
   _____ (53)

Thank you for completing and returning this questionnaire.

PRINTED IN U.S.A.

GABCD

NAME _____
        (Please Print)
ADDRESS _____
CITY _____
ZIP CODE _____

BUSINESS REPLY MAIL

FIRST CLASS   PERMIT NO. 717   BUFFALO, NY

POSTAGE WILL BE PAID BY ADDRESSEE

NATIONAL READER SURVEYS

901 Fuhrmann Blvd.
P.O. Box 1395
Buffalo, N.Y. 14240-9961

She climbed out of bed and padded down the hall to the guest room to shower and dress there. When she got downstairs, Cavan was already at the dining room table reading a newspaper. His breakfast was in front of him, but he had obviously waited for her before starting. Millie brought her a plateful of food, looking closely at her, trying to find any indication of what had happened between the newlyweds. She clicked her tongue in frustration as she left the dining room. They were both like stones, giving nothing away.

Meggie sensed Cavan's eyes on her, but it was a moment before she could look up with what she hoped was a carefree smile. "Do you have any plans for today?"

He looked at her for a long moment before answering, searching for some sign of the sadness he'd seen earlier and finding none. "Just work."

Meggie forced herself to eat some egg. "You mentioned that you were involved in several businesses last night. What kind?"

"I really don't think that's any of your concern."

His tone ended that line of conversation, but Meggie was nothing if not persistent, so she searched for a new one. "Have you seen the horses the Farrells own?"

"If you mean the horses I own, yes, I've seen them."

"They're beautiful. Are you going to keep them?"

"You're going to keep asking me questions until I answer one, aren't you?"

Meggie just smiled at him.

"All right. I am going to keep the horses. In fact, I'm going to breed them with some horses I own in the United States."

"I didn't know you were interested in anything like that."

His eyes met hers. "There's no reason why you would, Meghan."

Meggie's hurt eyes dropped to her plate as she concentrated on pushing a fried potato around. She felt as though he'd slapped her.

So did Cavan, and he hated himself for it. He'd hurt her twice today. Unintentionally, to be sure, but that made it no less real. "Meghan?"

She delicately cleared her throat and looked up.

"I'm sorry."

"There's no need to be, really."

"I don't apologize very often, so please don't throw this one away so lightly."

"I'm sorry."

A corner of his mouth lifted. "Now you've got the whole thing turned around."

Meggie smiled, responding to his teasing like a flower to sunlight, opening herself to him.

Cavan's eyes rested on her face. A delightful dimple creased her right cheek. Her hazel eyes sparkled with life and intelligence, and the whole picture was framed with her thick, shining auburn hair. God, she was lovely. "I'm leaving for America later this morning," he suddenly told her, having decided that very moment to make the trip.

"This morning?" She tried to think about what to pack. "How long will we be gone?"

"Not we, Meggie. I."

"Ah," she slowly nodded, "I should have known that. How long do you think you'll be gone?"

"I don't know."

Meggie's eyes looked into his, and her intuition told her that there was a woman involved somehow in this trip. His comely attorney, perhaps?

Cavan's eyes met hers, and he suddenly knew that she knew. He was discovering that Meggie's lovely, clear eyes were a mirror to her soul.

"May I ask you something?"

He waited.

"Why did you sleep with me last night?"

"It wasn't my intention. You were supposed to be in the guest room."

"Yes, but when you found me in your bed, you didn't leave and you didn't ask me to. Why?"

Millie came in at that moment to clear away the plates and Cavan waited until she'd gone before answering.

He gazed at her for a long moment. "Meghan, you asked me a question yesterday that I didn't have an answer for."

"Do you mean when I said now that you had me, what were you going to do with me?"

"That's right." He shook his head. "I haven't any idea. What are you expecting out of this marriage, Meghan?"

Oh, did she have an answer for that, but she didn't dare. Not yet. "I can't really define that, yet. We have an unusual situation, to be sure. I think for now I'd just like to make the best of it and see what happens."

"If this were a normal marriage, what would you want from it?"

"Oh, that's easy. To have a husband who loves me as much as I love him. To have his children."

"Those are simple dreams."

"Not from where I sit at this moment."

He inclined his head as her point registered. "What about a career?"

"I already have one that I'm very content with."

"As what?"

"A teacher at the orphanage."

"I didn't know that."

"There's no reason why you would," she gently tossed his words back to him.

A corner of his mouth lifted. "I can see that I'll have to be careful what I say to you."

"Only if you don't want to hear it again."

"About this job, is it volunteer work?"

"I don't need the money and they do need a teacher. Perhaps that doesn't seem as important to you as a career as a lawyer or a doctor would be, but I love what I do. I'm good at it."

"The children are lucky to have you."

"Thank you."

As Cavan looked at her, he realized that it would be easy for him to feel something for this woman if he'd let himself. But always between them was the fact that she was Padraic O'Neill's granddaughter. He couldn't see her without remembering those awful years in prison.

Meggie sensed Cavan's sudden withdrawal and wondered what she had said to cause it. Silence fell between them for a long moment. "Cavan? You never explained why you stayed with me last night."

His eyes rested on her lovely face. "Because you smelled wonderful," he said quietly. Then he set his napkin on the table and walked from the room.

Meggie sat back in her chair in surprise. So he was a little attracted to her after all. A small smile touched Meggie's mouth. Amazing how little it took to make her happy these days.

Still smiling, she reached across the table to get the newspaper Cavan had left behind and finished her breakfast.

Half an hour later Meggie looked at her watch. Taking a short drink of coffee, she dabbed at her mouth with her napkin and walked quickly into the foyer—and headlong into Cavan. He placed his hands on her shoulders to steady her. "Where are you going in such a hurry?"

"To work. And if I don't leave now I'll be late." She spotted his suitcase near the door. "I see you're packed. When are you leaving?"

"In a few minutes."

Her happy mood faded. "Oh. Where in America are you going?"

"Various places."

She looked into his eyes for a long moment. "I hope you have a nice trip."

"Thank you, Meghan."

"When will you be back?"

"I don't know."

She reached up and kissed him on the cheek. "Be safe."

And then Meggie left, trying hard not to look back. Afraid in her heart that he wouldn't come back at all.

Cavan stared at where she had stood long after she had gone. His hand rubbed the spot on his cheek where her mouth had rested so briefly.

Meggie kept herself so busy for the next few weeks that she dropped into bed exhausted every night, too tired to think about Cavan with some other woman, or to feel the loneliness she knew would engulf her if she let up. Since Cavan was interested in breeding horses, she went about investigating the lineage of the horses he'd won from Hugh Farrell and recording information about each of the animals that might be important. She worked around the house with Millie, tearing the place apart and giving it a cleaning like it hadn't had in decades, polishing the paneled walls and bookcases. She hired people to reupholster and re-drape in lighter colors and materials, and to generally let the sun into the house.

But one night even her labors didn't help her to sleep. She turned her head slightly on the pillow to glance at an illuminated clock on the bedside table. It was three o'clock in the morning, and she couldn't close her eyes without seeing Cavan's face or hearing his voice. She missed him so much it was a physical ache within her. What was he doing? Was he missing her at all?

Cavan glanced at his watch and sighed as he looked out over the couples in the elegant restaurant. Back in Ireland, where Meggie was, it was three o'clock in the morning.

"Cavan?"

His eyes came to rest on his mistress.

"Someone told me that you've been in the States for nearly three weeks, and here in New York for over ten days. Why haven't you called me before tonight?"

"I was here on personal business."

"I'm also your attorney."

"I know who you are, Jessica. If I had needed you for anything, I would have called."

She leaned back in her chair and studied him. "What's going on with you? Does it have something to do with that O'Neill girl?"

Meggie's lovely face flashed in his mind. "I'm married to her. It makes a difference."

"Why? Why should it? We both know your reasons for marrying her, and they had nothing to do with love."

"That's true. But I'm not going to make a fool of her. If nothing else, I owe her consideration," he echoed Meggie's words. "At least until we're not married anymore."

"And when will that be?" she asked quietly.

Cavan studied the rich red of the wine in his glass as it was illuminated by the candlelight. "I don't know. Right now there are a lot of things I don't know. Maybe when I've finished with her grandfather."

"That will only be a few more months. Ameri-Textiles is beating him in every market."

"Only because I'm pouring money into it."

"For whatever reason, his company is on its last legs. You've already won."

Cavan smiled, but there was no amusement in it. "For whatever it's worth."

"It's worth a lot. You can put this behind you forever as soon as you've divorced Meghan."

"I'm not going to divorce her."

Jessica sat straighter. "What do you mean?"

"Meghan is Catholic. If we get a divorce, she won't be able to marry again."

"So?"

"So she deserves a chance to start over when all of this is finished. I think an annulment is the answer."

"Since when did you develop a conscience?"

"Since I met Meghan O'Neill."

"If you're going to just turn her loose, what was the point in marrying her anyway?"

"To see the look on her grandfather's face when the priest spoke the words. That was my payback for his thinking I wasn't good enough for Caroline."

Jessica watched him closely. There was something different about him. "Have you fallen in love with her?"

Cavan said nothing as he sipped his wine.

"Have you?" she asked quietly.

"Jessica, what I feel or don't feel for my wife is between Meghan and me."

"All right. I respect that. But by the same token, I think how you and I feel about each other is strictly between the two of us. There's no reason to bring your wife into it." She leaned forward over the table more.

"Listen, Cavan, we're in New York. Your wife is in Ireland. She need never know about the two of us."

Cavan remembered the look in Meghan's eyes the morning he'd had breakfast with her. "She already does."

"You told her?" Jessica asked in amazement.

"I didn't have to. She has good instincts." Cavan inclined his head toward her plate. "Do you want anything else?"

She shook her head and Cavan signaled for the check.

"What's next?" she asked quietly.

"I take you home."

"And then?"

"I go back to my hotel—alone."

"We're good together, Cavan."

"We were, Jessica."

When he got to his hotel, he packed his suitcases and then picked up the phone to make a call.

Meggie jumped when the phone on the table by the bed rang. She picked it up and answered with a husky voice. "Hello?"

"Hello, Meghan."

Her heart lurched. "Cavan."

"Did I wake you?"

"No."

There was a pause. "I'm coming home."

Meggie closed her eyes. "All right."

"Goodbye, Meghan."

"Goodbye." She heard the click at the other end of the line, then fell back against her pillow hugging the receiver to her breast. He was coming home to her.

After Meggie got back from the orphanage the next day, she spent the afternoon working with Millie to get the house put back in order after all of the painters and paperhangers had cleared away their things. It looked like a completely new place where the sun was at last allowed to shine. In the drawing room where the carpeting had been a cranberry color and the drapes the same color in heavy velvet as befit a manor house of two hundred years, with fussily upholstered furniture, Meggie had started completely over with off-white carpeting and rich blue upholstery, echoing the same blue in the drapes that were pulled away from the windows to let in the light. Large plants brought the out-of-doors inside. The antique furniture scattered around the room didn't suffer in the least. If anything, the new simplicity enhanced the really fine pieces.

Millie lit a fire in the fireplace, and the two women stood back to admire their handiwork. "Do you think Cavan will like it?" Meggie asked.

"If he has any taste he will."

Meggie looked at her watch. "I wish I knew what time he was coming."

"Why don't you just get yourself cleaned up and dressed and then you won't have to worry about it?"

Meggie stripped the band from her ponytail and shook her hair free. "Once I slide into my bubble bath, you may never hear from me again."

"I know what you mean." The housekeeper rubbed the small of her back. "I hope pulling out all of the heavy old furniture isn't going to be a daily thing with you as mistress."

"Biannual."

Millie shook her head. "Even that makes me cringe."

"Maybe we should hire someone to co-housekeep with you."

"Male, about fifty, attractive, a little gray in his hair."

Meggie laughed. "Anything else?"

"Preferably single."

"I'll see what I can find."

"Speaking of which, if you don't need me for anything else this evening, I'd like to go out and do a little of my own looking."

"Go ahead. I want to cook dinner myself."

"I'll see you in the morning, then." And Millie went in one direction and Meggie in the other.

After her bath, Meggie stood in front of her closet and stared at her clothes. She wanted to look comfortably cute, yet sophisticated and a little sexy. A smile touched her mouth at the thought of what she expected from a mere dress.

Finally she decided to simply look like Meggie and slipped into a full emerald-green jacquard skirt and a white Edwardian blouse. She used makeup sparingly but well. Then she went downstairs and started cooking. First a mouth-wateringly delicious chicken curry, and rice to put it on, and fresh asparagus. Once Cavan got home, it would only take half an hour to get it on the table.

That done, she wandered into the drawing room and turned on some lights. The fire was crackling nicely. She tossed on another log and stood back to watch the flames lick around it.

Chimes rang in the front foyer. Meggie's heart flew into her throat. He was home! She took a deep breath and smoothed her skirt, then opened the door. A red-headed man with a cheerful, lopsided smile and freckles across the bridge of his nose looked her up and down appreciatively. "If only I'd known."

"Sean!" She hid her disappointment and hugged him. "What are you doing here?"

"Looking for a new, temporary residence." He reached down and lifted two large suitcases. "What do you think? Can you put me up until I find a place of my own?"

Her smile faded a little. "That might be a little awkward."

"I thought of that, but I couldn't think of anywhere else to go on such short notice. Do you mind if I come in?"

"Oh, Sean," Meggie moved away from the door, "I'm sorry. How rude of me."

He deposited his luggage against a wall near the door and walked on through to the drawing room where he stood looking around in surprise. "You've been busy."

Meggie came up behind him and looked as well. "Do you like it?"

"It's perfect—but Mother would have heart failure."

Meggie waved Sean onto the couch and took a chair across from him. "How is your mother?"

"Still not speaking to my father."

"I can hardly blame her."

"Personally, I think they both got what they deserved. I just found out today what they did to your husband."

Meggie looked at him in surprise. "Your mother was in on it?"

"She didn't help frame him, if that's what you mean, but she knew what was going on and didn't do anything to stop it."

"Cavan didn't have a chance, did he?"

Sean shook his head. "Speaking of Cavan, where is he? I'd like to speak with him."

"He's been in America for the past few weeks, but he's due back any minute. In fact, when you rang the doorbell I thought it was him."

"Sorry to disappoint you."

Meggie just smiled.

He looked at her curiously. "You know, Meggie, something has been bothering me about this marriage of yours."

"Such as?"

"When that contract was between the two of us, you wouldn't hear of it, even though we've been friends since childhood. Then this stranger comes along, wins the contract on a bet, mind you, and a week later you've married him without a whimper. I don't mind telling you that I'm a bit insulted and I'd like to know just what the hell's going on.''

"I happened to fall in love with him.''

"Just like that?''

"Just like that.''

He shook his red head. "Women.''

"Frustrating, aren't we?''

"Endlessly.'' He smiled at her. "But I'm glad you're happy, even if it isn't with me.''

"Thanks, Sean. Oh! I just remembered something that Millie and I came across on our rampage through the house. I was going to send it to your mother, but since you're here I'll just give it to you.'' She walked to a large table in a corner of the room and picked up a book that she brought back to Sean. "I can't imagine that she intended leaving it here.''

Sean opened the cover to find old photographs of himself and his family. He laughed as he pointed out one. "Look at this.''

Meggie sat next to him and smiled. "Do you think we were ever really that small?''

"It's hard to believe.'' He draped his arm lightly around her shoulders the way a close friend would.

"Oh, look at Caroline in this one.''

"Have you heard from her lately?''

Meggie shook her head. "I couldn't even contact her about my wedding.''

"That's too bad. I imagine she could have been helpful in giving you some insight into your husband.''

Meggie looked at him curiously. "What do you mean?''

Neither of them had noticed the man who entered the room behind them, watching; listening. "Meghan."

She rose so quickly she knocked the book from her lap. "Cavan!" Her eyes drank in the sight of him as he stood there, his sport coat suspended over his shoulder by a finger. He looked tired—as though he'd had as much trouble sleeping as she'd had. So intent were they on each other that Sean began to feel a little uncomfortable. He reached onto the floor to pick up the book of photographs, then rose and turned to face the man he had come here to see, his hand outstretched as he walked forward.

"Cavan Gallagher, I presume. I'm Sean Farrell."

Cavan looked at Sean's hand for a long moment before finally extending his own.

"I came here for a couple of reasons, the first of which is to apologize for my family."

Still Cavan said nothing, and Sean nervously shifted his weight onto his other foot.

"I also came to ask a favor, but this probably isn't the best time."

Cavan's eyes went over Sean's head to Meggie. "I'll see you in the library in a few minutes, Farrell."

Sean nodded a couple of times, a little slow to take the hint. But understanding eventually dawned. "Right." Then he did a crisp military turn and left the room.

As soon as he had gone, Cavan walked across the room to Meggie and placed a gentle finger under her chin, raising her face to his. His gaze roamed over every inch of it as though reassuring himself that he had remembered her correctly. Meggie's lips parted softly as her breathing grew deeper. Her breasts rose and fell noticeably beneath her high-necked blouse. Cavan's eyes rested on them for a moment, then moved back to her eyes. Then he wordlessly followed Sean's path to the library.

Meggie sank onto the couch, breathing as though she'd just run a marathon. She could physically feel her heart pounding. How could he do that to her with just a look?

When Cavan walked into the library, Sean jumped up from where he was sitting. Cavan waved him back down as he tossed his jacket over the back of a chair and leaned against the edge of the desk, his arms folded across his chest. "I heard what you were about to say to Meghan."

Sean looked at him blankly.

"About Caroline."

"I'm afraid I don't understand."

"Meggie doesn't know about Caroline and me."

"Then she doesn't know about her grandfather, either, does she?"

Cavan shook his head. "And I'd rather she didn't find out. It would hurt her."

"Sure it would, but don't you think she'll find out eventually anyway?"

Cavan just looked at him, and once again Sean felt twelve years old.

"Sorry."

"What is the favor you want?"

Sean cleared his throat. "Look, I feel strange about asking you this, but I need a place to stay. I have a flat picked out but it won't be available for a few weeks."

As Cavan looked at Sean, what he saw was Meghan's future after the annulment. "You can use the coach house."

Sean was pleasantly surprised. "Thanks. And I'll keep out of the way." There was an awkward silence. "If there's anything I can do to earn my keep, say the word."

"What do you know how to do?"

Sean gave a short laugh. "That's a good question, and one I've been asking myself recently. I've never had what you'd call a real job. But now I need one. There's no more family money." He thought for a moment. "I'm good with horses, but my only experience is with the ones here, and that's not enough to get myself a job."

"Good with horses in what way?"

"Horses respond to me. They train easier with me than with most people."

"Do you have any interest in horse breeding?"

"I do. I tried to get my father interested in it as a business—a way of shoring up the family's finances—but he never came around to my way of thinking."

"I have some horses in America that I'm having shipped here for breeding. How would you feel about working for me?"

Sean looked at him in surprise. "Me? Working for you?"

"On a trial basis. Free room and board and a reasonable monthly salary. We can try it for a couple of months to see how it works out."

"I'd like that a lot, thank you. My father will be furious, though."

"Is that a problem for you?"

"It used to be. It isn't anymore," he said as he rose and shook Cavan's hand. "I'll start tomorrow, first thing."

"You can't. The horses aren't here yet."

"Then I'll start as soon as they get here."

When Sean had gone, Cavan tiredly rubbed his forehead. He felt as if he could sleep for a week.

Meggie stood in the doorway. "Cavan?"

He looked up at her.

"Sean told me you're letting him stay here. That was nice of you."

He didn't say anything.

"Are you hungry?"

Again his eyes rested on her with blue intensity for a long moment before he answered. "Yes."

"I have some dinner made. It'll be ready in about half an hour."

"Where's Millie?"

"Trawling the pubs."

A corner of his mouth lifted. "Delicately put."

Meggie smiled also.

Cavan straightened away from his desk. "I'm going to take a shower, then I'll be down for dinner. Why don't you take some to Sean at the coach house. I don't imagine there's anything there for him to eat."

"All right."

He walked around the desk and past her. Meggie watched his disappearing back for a few minutes with a soft smile before going to the kitchen to put the finishing touches on the food. She fixed a plate for Sean and quickly walked it out to the coach house, but didn't stay to talk.

When she came back, she expected Cavan to be there, but he wasn't. She gave him a few more minutes, then went upstairs to see what was taking so long.

She found him still in the same clothes he'd had on earlier, stretched out across the middle of the bed, sound asleep.

She sat on the edge of the bed, a smile touching the corners of her mouth, as she reached out a gentle hand to touch his hair. He didn't move.

She rose quietly and walked to a chest at the foot of the bed and got out a blanket that she draped over him, then sat in a chair in a darkened corner of the room with her legs curled beneath her to watch her husband sleep.

He had come home.

For the first time since he'd left, Meggie felt at peace.

Chapter Five

When Meggie awoke the next morning, she was in bed. Alone. As she lifted her arms to stretch them over her head, she saw that she still had her blouse on. She must have fallen asleep in the chair and Cavan had laid her on the bed and covered her with a blanket. The thought made her smile.

With quick movements, she stripped and changed into a full, blue skirt, soft blue-and-white sweater and boots and went quickly downstairs. She found Cavan in the dining room finishing breakfast. Meggie quickly sat across from him. "Good morning," she said cheerfully.

He raised his eyes briefly from the newspaper. "Hello, Meghan."

The coolness of his tone surprised her, but she glossed over it. "You missed a fine dinner last night."

"It wasn't intentional. I hope you didn't go to too much trouble."

Looking like death warmed over, Millie walked in with Meggie's tea. Meggie watched in amazement as the housekeeper made it across the room holding herself so stiffly that she could have successfully carried a stack of posture books on her head. As she set the cup and saucer on the table, they rattled and Millie winced at the noise. "What would you like for breakfast?" she asked in a whisper.

"Nothing," Meggie whispered back.

"Bless you for the saint you are." Then she stiffly walked from the room.

"Oh," Meggie said sympathetically, "just watching her makes my head ache." She sipped her tea and studied her husband. "I'm sorry we didn't have a chance to talk last night. How did your trip go?"

Cavan looked up from the newspaper. His eyes rested on her for a long moment. He could tell her the truth. That he'd thought about her constantly, even when he'd tried not to. "All right." Then he looked at his watch and put his napkin on the table. "I'd like to talk to you later."

A small knot of apprehension tightened in Meggie's stomach at his serious tone. "About what?"

"The two of us. I'm going to be busy for most of the morning, so it'll have to be this afternoon, unless you have plans."

"I'm going riding with Sean this morning, but we should be back by one."

"You like Sean, don't you?"

"Of course," she said with a smile. "We grew up together."

"He seems like a good man."

"He is. One of the best. You'll like him when you get to know him."

"I take it he's nothing like his father."

"Not at all. I never cared much for Hugh, even before I found out what he did to you. Neither does Grandfather."

Cavan lifted a dark brow. "Your grandfather doesn't like Hugh Farrell?"

"Not at all. Hugh used to be a good friend of my father's when they were young. I guess they, in Grandfather's words, raised a lot of hell together."

"That's interesting. I guess that's why your father promised both of his daughters to Hugh's sons."

"Exactly. That also didn't thrill Grandfather."

"He wanted you to have free choice?"

"He would have preferred it, but one's given word is very important to him."

Cavan studied Meggie's fresh face. "You love your grandfather very much, don't you?"

"Oh, yes." A soft smile curved her mouth. "He's been mother and father to me since I was thirteen."

"I bet you were a handful," Cavan said quietly.

A dimple flashed in Meggie's cheek. "So I've been told. But he never complained. Well," she hedged, "almost never. He rather likes me the way I am."

Cavan rose from his chair and walked around the table, then leaned over and kissed the top of her head. "So do I. I'll see you later, Meghan."

She followed him from the room with her eyes, then leaned back in her chair with a contented sigh. A little more progress.

She sat quietly for a long time, sipping her tea and staring out the window, wondering what Cavan wanted to talk to her about. But that was an exercise in futility.

Meggie shook her auburn head and gathered up the dishes from the table.

Then she carried them into the kitchen where she found Millie sitting at the table pressing an ice pack to her head.

"Can I get you anything, Millie?" she asked sympathetically.

"A little plot behind the church might come in handy."

Meggie took a bottle of aspirin from the shelf and shook two into her hand, then got a glass of water and brought it to her housekeeper. Millie took the aspirin and stared at it. "This is like trying to bring down an elephant with a pellet gun."

Meggie dug her teeth into her lower lip to keep from laughing. "Why do you do this to yourself?"

"It was fun at the time. I'm too old for this, though. I ought to know better at my age."

"I think maybe you should spend the rest of the morning in bed until you're feeling better."

Millie adjusted her ice pack. "Bless you. You're..."

"A saint. I know."

"You are. But I can't possibly take the morning off. There's too much to be done. And the way I'm feeling is my fault entirely."

"That's true, but I still think you should get some rest, at least until you're feeling better." Meggie rinsed the plates off and dried her hands on a towel. "If anyone wants me for the next few hours, I'll be riding with Sean."

"With Sean?" Millie asked in surprise.

"He came by last night and needed a place to stay. Cavan let him have the coach house."

"How odd."

"It is, a little, I suppose. But it'll be nice to have him around. See you later."

As Meggie headed toward the stables, Sean caught up with her and slipped his arm through hers as they walked. "You might notice that I'm on time for a change."

"I did. What's gotten into you?"

"Something that should have gotten into me a long time ago. A sense of responsibility."

Meggie glanced at him in surprise. "I never thought I'd hear those words from your lips."

"I never thought I'd be saying them, but here I am. Yesterday I didn't have a place to live. Today I have a place to live and a job I'm looking forward to."

"Ouch!" Meggie stumbled and Sean caught her with his hands at her waist before she fell.

"What happened?"

Meggie was facing him, and rested her hand lightly on his shoulder as she rubbed her booted ankle. "I wasn't watching where I was going and stepped into a hole. What job?"

"I didn't go into it last night when you brought the food over because you were in a hurry, but your husband put me in charge of the stables. He's going to be breeding his American horses with the Irish ones here." His eyes shone with excitement. "This could be the start of something for me, Meggie. What an opportunity."

"You mean he hired you to work here?"

"That's right."

"I wonder why?"

Sean looked at her with wounded eyes. "Well, thank you for that vote of confidence, friend."

Meggie's smile was full of affection. "Oh, I didn't mean that. You know more about horses than anyone around here. I don't know why you haven't done anything about it before now. I was just thinking there had to be more to his hiring you than that."

"Why?"

"I don't know. It's just a feeling."

"Well, keep your feelings to yourself. I'm going to go on believing he hired me because he thinks I can do a good job. How's the foot?"

She gingerly put it on the ground and shifted her weight to it. "I think it's all right."

"Good. Let's go riding." He kissed the top of her head and wrapped his arm around her waist as they walked, the two of them comfortable in a way only two people who have known each other all their lives can be. "You know," Sean said after a moment, "it *is* a little ironic, if you think about it."

"What is?"

"Well, Cavan started out in my father's stables. Now I'm in the same stables, only I'm working for Cavan. Strange, how things turn out sometimes."

Cavan felt an unaccustomed tightening near his heart as he watched the couple disappear into the stables, but discounted it as the natural possessiveness of a man toward his wife whether he loved her or not. He slowly turned his large leather swivel chair away from the window and went back to work.

A few hours later, Meggie came happily into the house, her cheeks flushed, her hair disheveled from the ride. She stood in front of the closed library door for a moment and took a deep breath, trying to ready herself for whatever Cavan had to say. Finally she opened the door a crack and looked in. Cavan sat behind his desk, a file opened in front of him, a pen in his hand. "Hi."

He looked up from what he was doing and leaned back in his chair. "Come in, Meghan."

She sat in a chair across from him. "Sean told me you gave him a job. That was nice."

"I didn't do it because I was being nice. I did it because I think he can handle it."

"I stand corrected. What is it you wanted to see me about?"

"Our living arrangements."

"I don't understand."

Cavan tried to phrase it as carefully as he could to take the sting out of it. "I'd like us to try to maintain separate lives as much as possible. In all respects."

Meggie just looked at him for a moment. "But why?"

He tossed his pen onto the desk. "Look, Meghan, this marriage has gotten off to a rocky start. I think that until we figure out what we're going to do with each other, we ought to maintain a respectable distance."

"I thought we were. I mean one kiss in four weeks of marriage isn't exactly living on intimate terms."

Cavan smiled despite himself. "You cut right through to the basics, don't you?"

"I've found that it saves time and I'd appreciate it if you'd do the same."

The more Cavan was with Meggie, the more he liked her. "All right. I want to make sure that we don't ruin our chances for an annulment if things don't work out between us."

Her heart caught, but she did her best not to let him see that as her eyes searched his, trying to get at the meaning behind his words. "I see. Why don't you want to sleep with me, Cavan?"

"I do want to, Meghan. That's the problem."

"I'm afraid I don't understand."

"Once we cross that line, there'll be no chance of getting an annulment."

"I know that. I don't want an annulment."

He looked at her curiously. "But why not? There's no love between us."

"Yes, there is," she said quietly. "I've loved you for five years, ever since you picked me up out of the dirt where my horse deposited me. So if you want to live this marriage as though preparing for an annulment, do it for yourself, not for me."

She got to her feet. "If there's nothing else, I have some things I need to do."

Cavan stared after Meggie's disappearing back, and still stared when the door had closed behind her.

Meggie leaned back against the library door and closed her eyes. It was out in the open, but what must he think of her? Probably that she was some childish romantic.

She walked slowly back to the stables and found Sean still there, holding the receiver of a wall phone in his hand and staring at it with a frown.

She perched on the edge of a stall gate as he hung it up with a shrug and started brushing the horse he'd been riding earlier. "Who was it?"

"My father." Sean leaned his forearms on the back of the horse. "He's getting quite strange, Meggie. You'd think the most important issue in his life right now is how you and Cavan are getting on rather than how he's going to support himself and my mother."

"How Cavan and I are getting on? You think he's hoping for a separation so that you and I can get together?"

"That would be the normal thing, but that's not the impression I'm getting. He sounds almost as though he wants Cavan to fall in love with you."

"How odd."

Sean went back to brushing the horse, deep in thought, but then stopped again and looked at Meggie. "Tell Cavan to watch out for him, will you? Sometimes when my father drinks he becomes irrational."

"I will."

Sean looked at her more closely. "You seem distracted. Does that have something to do with Cavan?"

"It has everything to do with Cavan."

"Do you want to talk about it?"

"No." She smiled fondly at him. "But thank you for asking."

"You know, Meggie, contrary to what most of the townsfolk think, I know that yours is not a match made in heaven. You can talk to me and it won't go any further."

"I know that. I just don't want to talk to anyone. It's too personal."

"Even for the man you used to share a bathtub with?"

"We were two."

"You were two. I was four."

"Ah, yes, the older man in my life."

"That's right. And as the older man in your life, I think you should trust me enough to talk to me." There was a long silence, then, "You're in love with him, aren't you?"

She looked at him in surprise. "Is it that obvious?"

"To me."

Meggie plucked a brush from the wall, jumped off the gate and began helping to brush the horse. "Then you probably also noticed that Cavan and I have a very one-sided relationship."

"Probably a little less one-sided than you think."

"What do you mean?"

"Let's just say I saw the way he looked at you last night when he walked in the door."

Meggie looked at Sean over the horse's back. "Since when did you become so observant?"

"I've always been that way. You just never observed me while I was being observant." Sean shook his head. "Or something like that."

Meggie laughed as she brushed. But then she grew more serious. "You don't seem to hold any grudge against Cavan for what he did to your father."

"He didn't do anything to my dad that someone else wouldn't have done eventually."

"But this place was your inheritance."

Sean smiled, but there was no amusement in it. "For all it was worth. Cavan owned most of it before the card game. The only thing I'm going to inherit from my dad is debt. But at least now it won't be so overwhelming. Now that he doesn't own this place, people know his markers are worthless." He stopped brushing and looked at Meggie. "Cavan has given me a wonderful opportunity here, Meggie. I'm not angry with him. I'm grateful."

Meggie smiled at him, her eyes full of the sisterly love she felt for him. She had never seen Sean this excited about anything. Not even when they were children.

Sean saw the look and his heart caught. She had always been his Meggie. His friend. It was only just dawning on him that he loved her. And not the way a brother loves a sister.

He started brushing the horse again, harder than was necessary. "You must have better things to do with your time than brush down horses with me, Meggie. Go on back to the house."

She hung her brush up by its strap next to the stall and patted the horse on its silky neck. "Would you like to join us for dinner tonight?"

"No, thanks, Meggie. I have a lot of reading to do."

"About horses, no doubt."

"That's right. I already know a lot, but now I want to know everything."

"You have to eat."

"I know how to cook." Then he grinned at Meggie's skeptical look. "All right, I know how to make sandwiches. But that's all I want. Stop mothering me."

"You love it."

Suddenly his smile faded as he looked at her lovely face. "From my mother, Meggie. Not from you."

Meggie looked at him curiously. "What's wrong?"

Sean shook his head, and when he spoke, his voice was more calm. "Nothing. I was just thinking about something else."

"Anything I can help you with?"

A corner of Sean's mouth lifted, but there was no amusement in it. "Would that you could, Meggie. I didn't even know I had a problem until a little while ago. Just go back to the house."

Meggie watched him work for a moment, a frown creasing her forehead. What was bothering him all of a sudden? Without saying anything else, she left the stables and headed for the house. She found Millie in the kitchen, looking miserable. "You're *still* sick?"

"Worse than this morning."

Meggie touched Millie's forehead. "For heaven's sake, you're not hung over. You're ill." She went to a cabinet to get a thermometer, but Millie stopped her.

"Please," she lifted her hand and then let it fall limply back onto the table, "I don't want to know how high it is."

"Well at least let me help you to bed."

"But what about dinner?"

Meggie put her arm under Millie's elbow and raised her out of the chair. "Ireland has enough martyrs without your name being added to the list. I'll fix dinner."

"We need groceries."

"I'll go shopping."

Millie started for the door, not standing nearly as straight as she usually did. "There was something I was supposed to tell you.... Oh! Father Flaherty called from the Kilgarrin Orphanage to tell you that little Sarah isn't feeling well and is asking for you."

"What's wrong with her?"

"The flu or some such thing. It didn't sound very serious."

"Good. Let's get you to bed and then I'll head over there."

"I can get myself to bed, but I'd appreciate a cup of tea."

"All right. I'll bring it up in a minute."

When Millie had gone, Meggie made the tea and put it, along with some warm toast, on a tray and carried it upstairs. Millie was already under the covers when Meggie got there. "Where do you want it?"

TAKE **4 FREE** BOOKS
WHEN YOU PEEL OFF THE BOUQUET
AND SEND IT ON THE POSTPAID CARD

Silhouette ◗ *Romance*®

Debbie Macomber's CHRISTMAS MASQUERADE. Jo Marie met Andrew at the Mardi Gras. By Christmas, he was introduced to her as someone else's fiancé. Why, she wondered, didn't he seem happy with his intended? Why was she back in his arms tonight? Could Andrew still be her dream man?

Arlene James' NOW OR NEVER. Mary Judith could sense new handyman Nolan Tanner was hiding a secret. She also knew one touch from him could unlock her own fiery passions. Living under the same boarding-house roof made their love seem so right — if only she could discover his secret.

Emilie Richards' GILDING THE LILY. Lesley had always held back — from success, from men, from love. Now, she had a chance to interview Travis Hagen, America's premier cartoonist. One look, and one kiss, from Travis and Lesley knew her days of holding back were gone forever.

Rita Rainville's WRITTEN ON THE WIND. Handwriting analyst Dena Trevor has to convince acting company president Brand McAllister that her expertise can unmask a company spy. Level-headed Brand has to convince himself that he is not falling in love with the beautiful Dena.

OPEN YOUR DOOR to these exciting, love-filled, full-length novels. They are yours *absolutely FREE* along with your Folding Umbrella and Mystery Gift.

AT-HOME DELIVERY. After you receive your 4 FREE books, we'll send you 6 more Silhouette Romance novels each and every month to examine FREE for fifteen days. If you decide to keep them, pay just $11.70 — with no additional charges for home delivery. If not completely satisfied, just drop us a note and we'll cancel your subscription, no questions asked. **EXTRA BONUS:** You'll also receive the Silhouette Books Newsletter FREE with every book shipment. Every issue is filled with interviews, news about upcoming books, recipes from your favorite authors, and more.

"On the end table here. I'll get to it in a few minutes."

Meggie checked her forehead again. "Do you think you need a doctor?"

"To tell me to take some aspirin and go to bed? Not hardly."

"All right," Meggie grinned. "I'll check on you when I get back from the orphanage."

"I'll be here."

Meggie went to her room and changed out of her riding clothes and into a full wool skirt and bulky sweater, then picked up her purse and car keys and headed downstairs.

Cavan was walking past the stairs, but stopped when he saw her. Meggie's heartbeat accelerated as she closed the gap between them, wondering what he was thinking now that he knew how she felt about him.

"Where are you going?"

"To the orphanage. Sarah's sick."

"I hope it's nothing serious."

"It doesn't sound like it."

"When will you be back?"

"I don't really know, but it shouldn't be too late."

Cavan had a strange feeling he couldn't explain that Meggie shouldn't be going out alone. "I think you should take someone with you. Maybe Sean."

"Sean has other things to do. Besides, there's no reason I can't drive to the orphanage by myself. I do it every day."

"If you won't take Sean, I'll come myself."

Meggie looked at him curiously. "Why? I really don't need a baby-sitter."

"It's dark out, Meghan. You shouldn't be going out alone."

She had to admit that his concern for her safety was nice to hear. "This is Ireland," she said with a soft smile. "Nothing is going to happen to me. Besides, I know a great shortcut. I'll be there in no time."

He still didn't like it, but it was obviously a waste of time to argue with her.

Suddenly she stood on her tiptoes and kissed him on the cheek. "Goodbye. I'll call before I come home." She started to leave, but turned at the door with a smile playing at the corners of her mouth. "And thank you for worrying."

Cavan's eyes followed her out the door. Meggie was getting to him. He knew it. It was impossible to keep his distance. She wouldn't let him—and he wasn't sure he wanted to anymore. Why couldn't he just relax and let himself fall in love with her? It would be so easy.

Meggie sped off in her little car. The shortcut to the orphanage was more than a hundred years old and worn out from decades of neglect. Meggie usually traveled a more widely used highway when she went there, but this route would cut fifteen minutes from her driving time. She dodged the holes she knew were there, but the darkness made it difficult to spot the rough areas, and the beams from her headlights bouncing wildly over the landscape didn't help any.

Finally she spotted the lights of the old gray stone building that had once been a castle and a moment later parked in front of it. Father Flaherty met her at the door with an apologetic smile. "Sorry to drag you out like this."

"I don't mind. How is she?"

"She'll be fine in a couple of days. This is the first time she's really been sick since her parents, God rest their souls, were killed. I think she just needs a little extra coddling and we haven't the resources here to do it. Several of the other children are sick also."

"Is she in her usual room?"

At the priest's nod, Meggie climbed the winding stairs to the next floor and walked down the long hall to a half-open door. She went quietly in and found Sarah asleep in her bed, clutching her doll. Meggie leaned over and gently pushed Sarah's curly hair from her damp forehead. Black lashes rested on flushed cheeks still a little round with baby fat.

Slowly, Sarah opened her eyes and focused on Meggie. A soft smile touched her mouth as she reached up to take Meggie's hand, then she promptly fell back asleep. Meggie held her hand until she got tired of standing, then gently laid her little hand on top of the sheet and pulled a chair near the bed. There was something about Sarah that touched her in a way no other child ever had.

The bedside lamp was flickering a little. After a while it annoyed Meggie and she got up to tighten the bulb, then went to the narrow window and stood looking down at the courtyard. She loved this place. It was a typical castle, with fireplaces in every room and bathrooms down the hall. It could have been an austere place, but the nuns who lived here had turned it into a place to delight children with bright wallpaper and pictures hanging everywhere. It was often damp and chilly, which was more the price one paid for living in Ireland than living in an old castle. The school at which Meggie taught was a large room in a wing north of where she was at the moment.

From the school windows she could see the gardens where the older children worked and learned. Everyone pitched in at the orphanage in one way or another to keep the castle and its grounds in shape. The people of Kilgarrin would make clothes for the children sometimes, and pass along hand-me-downs. Nothing went to waste around here.

"Meggie?"

She inhaled sharply and turned away from the window, her hand over her heart. "Oh, Father Flaherty, it's you."

"Sorry I startled you, girl. How's Sarah? Does she know you're here?" he asked as he walked over to the bed and looked down at her.

Meggie joined him. "She woke for a moment when I first came in, but she hasn't stirred since. I think I'll spend the night in case she needs me."

"Stay for a time, certainly, but not all night. Tomorrow is when she'll be wanting you."

Meggie touched Sarah's soft hand again. "She's so sweet."

"She is that." He looked at her from the corner of his eye. "So why don't you and Cavan adopt her?"

Meggie grew thoughtful. Adopting Sarah had occurred to her, but with things the way they were between Cavan and herself, Sarah was going to have to wait. "Maybe someday, Father."

"As long as you're thinking about it, I won't harass you. You're coming to the ball this year, aren't

you? The children have worked especially hard on the
castle ballroom."

"Is it that time of year already?" Meggie asked in
amazement. Every year the orphanage sponsored a
ball to raise money for the children and to allow people to enjoy themselves while emptying their pockets
at the same time. "I guess I did hear the children
chattering about it, but it didn't register."

"It's exactly a week from tonight. Have that husband of yours bring his checkbook. And while you're
at it, bring your own."

"I always do."

He winked at Meggie and patted her shoulder.
"Well, I'm off now. I have some other calls to make
tonight. One of them is on your grandfather."

"For chess?"

"I hope so. His heart hasn't been in his game for the
past few weeks, though. I've been able to beat him
handily."

"I think he's still upset about my marriage."

"That he is. No one is good enough for you in his
eyes."

"When he gets to know Cavan better he'll change
his mind."

Father Flaherty kissed her cheek. "I hope so, child.
I'll probably be seeing you tomorrow morning."

"Goodbye," she said quietly.

When the priest had gone, Meggie sat back in the
chair and watched Sarah. She woke a few times during the next several hours, and each time seemed
happy to have Meggie with her.

"Meggie?" a soft voice whispered from the doorway.

She turned to find a nun there.

"Father Flaherty asked me to make sure you went home tonight. It's nearly one in the morning."

Meggie looked at her watch and rose. "I had no idea. I'll be on my way in a minute."

She inclined her head and left.

Meggie gently kissed Sarah's forehead. "I'll be back first thing in the morning," she said softly. "Before you wake."

Then she left the room and went to the office on the main floor to use the phone. After she dialed, she waited.

"Yes." It was Cavan's voice, and a warm feeling washed through Meggie the way she imagined it always would when she heard him.

"Hello, Cavan. It's Meggie. I just wanted to tell you that I'm on my way home. I'm using that shortcut I told you about, so I shouldn't be too long."

"I'll come to get you."

"That's not necessary."

"Meghan, I don't want you driving home alone this late at night."

"I'll be fine. I only called because I said I would, but there's no need for you to worry. See you soon." And she hung up.

A short time later she was back on the wretched road, bumping her way back the way she had come. A few times she was sure she was going to be swallowed by a pothole, but the little car always seemed to find its way out. But one of the holes was more lethal than the others. The minute the front tire hit it, Meggie knew she was in trouble. She heard the blowout. She was going faster than she should have been and her brakes locked on the mist-slick road, sending the little car hurtling into a ditch.

When the car finally jolted to a halt, Meggie just sat there for a minute, absolutely still. The intense silence after the noise of the crash was hypnotic. She unfastened her safety belt and tried the door. It was jammed, so she hit it with her shoulder a few times but it wouldn't give. She pressed the switch for the power windows but nothing happened.

"Wonderful," she said out loud to herself. "Just wonderful."

She climbed to the other side of the car and tried the passenger door, but it was jammed as well. There was absolutely nothing she could do but sit there and wait to be rescued—and on this road, who knew how long that would take? She hadn't passed anyone either coming or going.

Ten minutes later, as she sat in the darkened car, she sniffed at a strange smell that drifted in. Then with a little frown, she sniffed again. Fuel! Her car was leaking fuel! Meggie struggled with the doors again. The one on the driver's side gave a little, but not enough for her to get out.

And then, as Meggie watched in trapped horror, she saw the fire start. It began with a little flash when the fuel got to the hot engine and then spread under the car. "No!" she screamed. "Help! Somebody help me, please!"

Suddenly Cavan was there, outside the window, pulling on the door until the metal got too hot for his hands. He ran back to his car and got something from the trunk used for changing tires and tried to pry open Meggie's door. A strange calm filled her as she watched the sweat glisten on his intense face in the firelight. There was the heavy groan of metal fighting metal. Moments later the door was open and Cavan reached in and dragged Meggie from the car, holding her hand and pulling her along behind him toward the safety of his car. But before they got there, an ear-shattering explosion rocked the ground they ran on. Cavan tackled Meggie, covering her body with his own to protect her from the debris that fell around them. There was another explosion and another, and then the fire burned with crackling intensity. Smaller fires started by the rain of debris were like little campfires dotting a fifty-yard circle around what was once her car.

Cavan rolled off of Meggie and looked down into her soot-streaked face. "Are you all right?"

"Thanks to you. How did you come to be here, anyway?"

"I had a bad feeling so I decided to meet you halfway, just to make sure nothing happened."

Meggie turned her head slightly and looked at the flames, shivering when she realized how close she had come to being in there.

Cavan had the same thought. Suddenly his mouth came crushingly down on hers. Both of them were still out of breath from running, and it made the kiss seem all that more desperate. Meggie's lips parted softly, welcoming him. Her fingers tangled in his thick hair, pulling his mouth even more firmly against hers.

But then the desperation faded. His kiss grew more gentle, more probing. He raised his head to gaze down at her and gently pushed her hair away from her face as though he were seeing the woman he married for the very first time. "Oh, Meghan," he groaned just before his mouth captured hers again, "what have you done to me?"

Meggie's breathing grew erratic again, but it had nothing to do with running from the fire. Cavan's mouth moved across the clean line of her jaw to the sensitive spot behind her ear and lingered there, teasing. His warm breath brushed her ear as his hand slipped down the side of her body and came to rest on the curve of her hip. He rolled onto his side, bringing Meggie with him, pulling her hips tightly against his until she could feel his desire pressing against her. Meggie slipped her hands beneath his shirt and ran her fingers over his smoothly muscled back as she rubbed her body suggestively against his, delighting in the way he sharply inhaled, knowing that he wanted her at this moment as much as she wanted him.

Cavan's mouth recaptured Meggie's as he rolled her gently onto her back. His hand moved under her sweater across the soft, warm flesh of her stomach to gently massage her breast. Meggie moaned against his mouth, loving what he was doing, but wanting more.

Both of them heard the siren in the distance. Meggie tried to ignore it, but Cavan was more practical. A corner of his mouth lifted as he looked down at her.

"It looks like help is arriving," he said in a voice husky with desire.

"How timely."

His smile grew larger and he pulled Meggie's sweater back into place, then rose, bringing Meggie up with him. "Remember where we left off."

Meggie wobbled a little and Cavan wrapped his arm protectively around her shoulders as the police car pulled up, lights flashing, siren suddenly silent. "What happened here?" he asked as he climbed out of his car and made his way to the couple standing near the road.

"I hit a pothole, got a flat tire, lost control of my car and—" she waved toward the diminishing flames "—you see what happened."

"I'd like to take my wife home," Cavan told him. "She's explained pretty much what happened. If you have any other questions, perhaps you could ask them tomorrow."

"As long as you were the only one involved, I suppose that would be all right. What's your name, ma'am?"

"Meggie O'Neill."

"Gallagher," Cavan corrected.

"Gallagher," the officer said thoughtfully. "You live in what used to be the Farrell house, don't you?"

"That's right."

"Well, lucky you," he said sarcastically. "Imagine being a thief one minute, and moving into your victim's house the next."

Meggie was too shocked by his words to say anything, but Cavan seemed to take it in stride. "As I said, if you have any questions, my wife will speak with you tomorrow." And with that he guided Meggie to his car.

When he climbed into the driver's seat next to her, Meggie studied his carved profile. "How can you let him talk to you like that?"

Cavan put the car into gear and concentrated on maneuvering through the potholes. "He didn't say anything I haven't heard before."

Meggie was appalled.

"No matter where I go, the past haunts me. It's not something you ever get used to, but after a while you learn to ignore the remarks. What's worse than that is being hauled into police stations every time there's a robbery within a hundred miles of where I am."

"I'm so sorry."

Suddenly Cavan stopped the car and turned in his seat to look at Meggie. "You have nothing to be sorry about. If anyone should be apologizing, it's me, for dragging you into the middle of this mess. I was wrong to do it." He trailed his fingers down her smooth cheek. "You've become as much my victim as I was of your...of Hugh Farrell."

"You're wrong, Cavan," she said quietly. "I'm not your victim. I'm married to you because I choose to be, not because I was forced into it."

Cavan knew in that moment that he could never tell her what her grandfather had done. He could never hurt her like that. Cavan Gallagher was most definitely falling in love with his wife. He leaned forward and kissed Meggie on the forehead. "Let's get you home." He started the car again and they drove the rest of the way in silence, with Meggie's eyes on her husband.

When they got to their house, an unfamiliar car was parked in the drive. "Oh, no," Meggie sighed. "Who could it be at this hour?"

"Your guess is as good as mine."

The two of them wearily climbed to the top of the steps. Suddenly the door flew open and an elegant woman with short blond hair stood looking at the two of them.

Cavan's eyes narrowed on her, but Meggie ran up the last step and threw her arms around her sister. "Caroline!"

Chapter Six

W hat are you doing here?" Meggie asked.

"You're asking me that? I go on a short vacation and when I return it's to find you married and living in this house." She turned her eyes on Cavan, who stood quietly watching the two sisters. "Hello, Cavan."

He inclined his head, then stepped past her into the house, bringing Meggie with him. "Meghan, I think you should go clean up. I'll keep your sister company until you've finished."

Meggie hugged Caroline again. "Whatever you do, don't leave until I come back down. We have a lot of catching up to do."

Caroline's narrowed blue eyes followed Meggie up the staircase. "We certainly do."

Cavan took Caroline's arm and led her into the library where he closed the door behind them. "You and I need to talk."

"About what? Did you pick the wrong sister?"

Cavan looked at her for a long moment. "Not this time, Caroline," he said coolly.

She lifted a skeptical brow. "I know exactly why you married Meggie. It was to get back at me for choosing Tom over you."

"You didn't choose Tom Farrell over me. Your father threatened to cut you off without a penny if you didn't do as he said. You chose your inheritance over me."

"All right, I'll concede the point. But why did you marry Meggie?"

"It started out as revenge on your grandfather."

"And now?"

He ran his hand through his hair as he remembered the horror he'd felt when he saw her in that burning car. "I care about her very much, and I don't want her to get hurt."

"What does she know?"

"It's what she doesn't know that's more important."

"Which means she doesn't know about the two of us, or about Grandfather. Don't you think she should be told?"

"About you and me, yes, and I'll tell her when the time is right, but I don't think she needs to know about Padraic."

"She's going to find out anyway. I did."

He looked at her curiously. "When?"

"About a year ago, right after my husband died, I was here with Hugh and Sean. Hugh had too much to drink, as usual, and started reminiscing. He was talking about how hard he had worked with my family to get Tom and me married and how easy it had been to set you up." Caroline touched his arm. "I'm sorry, Cavan, but until that moment, I honestly thought you'd taken the jewels."

"So did everyone else."

"I suppose I should have been appalled by what Grandfather did, but I think having just lost my husband cushioned the shock. I needed him then and he was there for me. I've never even discussed it with him."

"But Meggie isn't you."

"I know. And she's a lot closer to him than I was. He raised her, whereas I was already married with a home of my own when our parents died."

"That's why I don't want her to know. It would hurt her too much. She'd never be able to forgive him, and that would leave a terrible void in her life." He shook his head. "I still haven't figured out how she escaped hearing about the two of us."

"The people in Kilgarrin aren't gossips, and Meggie was away at school when all of this was going on. She knows something happened ten years ago, but not what."

"Why didn't you ever tell her?"

Caroline shrugged her shoulders. "I'm six years older than she. She was only twelve at the time and by the time she was old enough for me to want to confide in, it was a part of my past I didn't want dredged up anymore, particularly since you were in prison.''

Meggie, freshly scrubbed and changed, looked around the library door and then came fully into the room. ''There you are!''

As Cavan's eyes came to rest on her, he was amazed by the warm contentment that washed over him.

''Are the two of you getting reacquainted?''

Caroline looked at her curiously. ''How did you know we knew each other?''

''Cavan mentioned it the first time we met.''

''Then I guess the answer is yes, we're getting reacquainted. Do either of you know what time it is?''

Cavan looked at his watch. ''Two-thirty.''

''Two-thirty! What a ridiculous hour. I have to be getting back to Grandfather's. He'll be worried.''

''You could call him,'' Meggie suggested.

''Thanks, but no, sis. I've had a long day and I think I'd like to fall into bed until about noon. I'll see you sometime tomorrow and we can get all caught up then.'' She hugged Meggie and then kissed Cavan's rough cheek.

''I'll walk you out,'' Meggie offered. ''Cavan?''

He hadn't taken his eyes from Meggie since she'd walked into the room. ''I'll wait here for you, Meghan.''

When she came back a few minutes later, she found him staring out the library window into the inky night. ''Have you had dinner?'' she asked, feeling suddenly shy.

''I wasn't hungry. What about you?''

''I didn't have any, but I'm not hungry either.''

Cavan grew silent for a long time. "Meghan, you and I need to talk about what happened between us earlier."

A shy smile touched Meggie's mouth.

Cavan stood in front of her and cupped her face in his hands as his eyes gazed tenderly at her. "You have done nothing but delight me since our marriage. Everything I learn about you, everything I see in you, makes me want to love you."

"I hear a 'but' coming."

Cavan smiled at her and pulled her into his arms. His breath ruffled her silky hair. "But it's too soon, Meghan. You know almost nothing about me."

"I don't need to know anything else," she said quietly.

He held her a little closer and Meggie melted against him. She had never felt safer. Never happier. She was exactly where she belonged. "But you do, Meghan."

"Why?"

Cavan moved slightly away so that he could look down at her. "I feel as though I've been given this wonderful gift and I can't accept it. You and I are such different people. We've lived such different lives. You're open and warm and giving."

"And you're not?"

His eyes rested on her lovely mouth. "And I'm not," he said softly.

"But you can be when you want to."

"I can also be a son of a—"

Meggie pressed her fingertips lightly against his mouth. "Stop trying to talk yourself out of me. I won't let you do it."

"You'd be better off with Sean."

"If I'd wanted Sean I would have married him and not you."

Cavan had to resist the urge to carry her off to his room. "It's important, for your sake, Meghan, that we're both absolutely sure about what's happening between us before we do anything about it."

Meggie knew what he was saying. "I'm already sure."

"But I'm not. And as you get to know me better, perhaps you won't be either." He touched the shadows beneath her eyes. "You look so tired."

"I am. And I have to get up early in the morning and go back to the orphanage."

"How is Sarah?"

"She'll be fine. It's just the flu." She hesitated for a moment. "Father Flaherty made an interesting suggestion tonight."

"Which was?"

"That you and I adopt Sarah."

"And you said?"

A dimple touched her cheek. "Not much."

"We're a long way from having children."

"Ah, but Sarah's already arrived—and with no pleasant effort on our part."

Cavan shook his head, but he was anything but angry. "She means a lot to you, doesn't she?"

"I love her. And having now confessed all, I'm going to bed. This has been a long day."

"Good night, Meghan," he said quietly. "Sweet dreams."

She turned at the door, an impish twinkle behind her hazel eyes. "I don't suppose you'd consider a platonic cuddle with your wife, would you?"

A corner of Cavan's mouth lifted. "Can't be done. Ask me again in thirty years."

Meggie's smile grew broader, and then she left.

Cavan turned out the lights and lay on the couch, one arm behind his head, as he looked up at the ceiling. Things were becoming more and more complicated. When he had been planning his revenge, he never figured on falling in love with his wife. But if he'd learned anything tonight, it was that he was indeed falling in love with Meggie. So where did he go from here? He couldn't very well continue calmly destroying her grandfather's livelihood.

And what was going to happen when she found out what her grandfather had done? Meggie wasn't predictable.

And in his heart he knew that one day she'd find out. Secrets like that had a way of making themselves known.

Meggie was up early the next morning before anyone else. She dressed in a full green corduroy skirt and V-necked sweater with a white blouse beneath, then went running to the coach house to rouse Sean from a sound sleep.

When he opened the door, he stood squinting down at her. "Do you have any idea what time it is, Meggie?"

"Six o'clock. I need to borrow your car."

"Where's yours?"

"It blew up last night."

"Hey, if you don't want to tell me, just say so." He walked back into the house and returned a moment later with a set of keys. "I need it back by this afternoon."

"No problem. Thank you."

He watched her run back across the lawn and shook his head. How could anyone move at that hour, much less run? It was barbaric. Scratching his head, he went back into the house and closed the door.

Meggie used the main road this time to drive to the orphanage. It was a beautiful morning. The air was crisp and clear. She rolled down the window and let the wind whip her hair around. She was so happy it was hard to stop smiling. Things with Cavan were going better than she would have expected after only a month of marriage. They just might make it.

When she got to the orphanage, she found Father Flaherty at the foot of the stairs. "Good morning!"

"Morning, Meggie. What brings you back here so early?" Then he lifted his hand. "Sarah, of course. Sorry. My mind isn't working very well at this hour."

"Have you seen her yet?"

"No. Just got here myself. Come on," he caught her hand in his, "I'll walk you up." He looked at her sideways as they climbed the stairs. "You seem awfully cheerful this morning."

"Do I?"

"And mysterious."

"I don't think I've ever been called that before."

They came to Sarah's room and went in. The little girl was still sleeping. Meggie leaned over and kissed her forehead. "She's cooler today."

"To be sure. She's fine. The flu doesn't take all that long to get over when you're three."

Meggie sat in the same chair she'd pulled near the bed the night before. Father Flaherty rested his hand on her shoulder for a moment. "If you'll excuse me, I'm going to look in on the other children."

Suddenly Cavan appeared in the doorway behind the priest. "Hello, Father."

"Cavan." They shook hands. "We weren't expecting you. Perhaps we can talk later."

Meggie smiled at Cavan after the priest had gone. "Good morning."

"Good morning." He moved next to Meggie and looked down at the little girl. "How is she?"

"She seems fine. What are you doing here?"

"I intended to drive you here this morning, but you got up before I did."

"I borrowed Sean's car."

"So he told me. How long are you going to stay at the orphanage?"

"For the day. I'll be teaching a little later, and after that I thought I'd come back here and keep Sarah company."

"Then I probably won't be seeing you for a couple of days."

"Where are you going?"

"I have some business in the north to attend to. I'll be back as soon as I've finished."

Meggie's disappointment shone from her eyes. "I wish you weren't going."

"I do, too, to be honest, but it can't be helped." Sarah stirred and they both grew quiet for a moment. "Do you remember my attorney, Jessica . . ."

"Pierson," Meggie finished for him. "Yes, I remember her. Why?"

"She's due here in a few days. There are some business details we need to take care of. I'd appreciate it if you could find a place for her to stay until I get back."

"How about one of the guest rooms?"

"I think a local hotel would be a better idea." He didn't elaborate, but Meggie knew what was going on, and she could have kissed him for it. She wasn't sure she could look at Jessica morning after morning, knowing what she knew.

Cavan stood behind Meggie's chair and Meggie leaned her head back against him and looked up. "I'm going to miss you."

"As soon as I get back, we'll go out for dinner."

"I'd like that. A date with my husband."

"We have to start somewhere." He kissed the top of her head. "I'll call you if I'm going to be longer than I said. Goodbye."

"Bye."

Meggie felt wretched after he left. With a sigh, she went to the window and looked outside. Cavan's car was parked next to Sean's. As she watched, Cavan walked across the courtyard and climbed into his. Her eyes followed his car down the road until it disappeared from sight. Her happy mood of a little earlier faded. She wasn't looking forward to dealing with

Jessica. One of these days the woman was going to have it out with her. She could feel it coming.

When she finally got home she found Caroline waiting for her on the steps. "It's about time you got home. School was out ages ago."

"I had some errands to run."

"Ah, I forgot, you're a married woman now." Caroline smiled at her. "I have such a hard time picturing you as someone's wife. You've always been my baby sister. But enough of that. Get some riding clothes on. I haven't been on a good horse in months."

"You should spend more time in Ireland."

Caroline looked around and her eyes grew soft. "It is beautiful here. I'm sure Millie thinks I'm crazy," she said as she got to her feet and brushed off her riding pants, "because I wanted to wait for you outside, but it's peaceful here. I'm tired of being cooped up in hotel rooms."

Meggie led the way inside and started up the stairs. "I'll be right back." She changed quickly into a pair of jeans and a warm sweater, pulled her hair back into a heavy ponytail and ran back downstairs where she found her sister in the living room staring out the window. "I'm ready."

Caroline turned and looked her up and down. "How anyone can look that good in old jeans and a baggy sweater, I'll never know. Come on."

When they got to the stables, they each chose a horse and saddled them themselves. "Where shall we ride to?" Meggie asked, swinging herself up and adjusting her seat.

Caroline swung herself up as well. "Someplace beautiful. I feel like drinking it all in before I have to go back to London." Then she kneed her horse and it shot through the stable doors and across the pasture with Meggie's horse a close second.

"Why are you going back?" Meggie called out when she'd caught up.

"That's where I live."

"Move back here. There's no reason not to now that Tom is gone. I miss you. So does Grandfather."

Caroline pointed to a small hill about half a mile away. "I'll race you to the top!" Then she kneed her horse and pulled ahead of Meggie.

Meggie kneed her own horse and caught up with Caroline a few seconds later and they raced neck and neck until they reached the top at the same time. Both of them slid from their horses and sat under a dying tree trying to catch their breath while the animals grazed nearby. "I'll never understand why people get so winded when they race horses," Meggie panted. "The horses do all the work."

"Are you kidding? Clinging for dear life takes a lot of energy."

They both grew quiet, happy in each other's company as they looked out over the green pastures separated at intervals by low stone walls. Then Meggie glanced at her sister. "My instincts tell me that there's a reason behind this sudden urge of yours to go riding."

"You know me too well," Caroline said with a smile. "There is something I want to talk to you about. I think Cavan would have eventually told you, but to my way of thinking, this is something between sisters."

"This sounds serious."

"It is, a little. It concerns Cavan and me."

Meggie waited, not sure she wanted to hear what was coming.

"Do you remember a time about ten years ago when I was having some trouble at home?"

"Vaguely. You didn't want to marry Tom, or something like that."

"Something exactly like that. Cavan was the reason."

Meggie's mouth parted softly in surprise. "Cavan? My Cavan?"

"He wasn't yours at the time, if you'll recall," she said dryly. "I thought I was in love with him. I tried to talk to our parents about it, but they wouldn't listen. Their daughter with a common stablehand? And one who was American-Irish, no less, rather than full-blooded."

"So what did you do?"

"We ran off together to be married."

Meggie grew quiet. "Cavan must have loved you very much."

Caroline shook her head. "No. We were emotional children who didn't know the meaning of the word."

"So that's why Hugh set up Cavan with that jewelry," Meggie said thoughtfully. "To keep him from running off with you, and incidentally his security for the future. And that must also be why there's such animosity between Cavan and Grandfather."

Caroline said nothing. She agreed with Cavan about Meggie not needing to know about their grandfather.

Meggie looked over at her sister. "How do you feel about Cavan now?"

A corner of Caroline's mouth lifted. "You want the truth?"

"I'm not so sure, when you put it like that."

"Well, I'm going to give it to you anyway. He's wonderful, and if I thought I had a chance with him, I'd take it in a minute. But he's not interested. What would you do if I *was* after him?"

"Fight like hell."

Caroline smiled as she lay back on the grass next to her sister. "That's what I thought."

They both grew quiet. "Do you think," Meggie finally asked, "that Cavan married me as a way of punishing you?"

"I did when I first heard about it. I was quite flattered, actually. Then I made the mistake of asking him."

Meggie turned her head and studied her sister's profile. "What did he say?"

"That this time he had the right sister."

Meggie's smile lit her entire face. "That's wonderful. Thank you for telling me."

"I rather thought you'd like that."

Still smiling, Meggie stared up at the blue sky. "I wonder why Cavan didn't tell me himself."

"As I said before, I think he intended to. He just hasn't gotten around to it yet."

Meggie rolled onto her stomach and propped her chin up on her hand. "You know, Caroline, I think he's falling in love with me."

"So do I," she said softly.

"I have some competition, though."

"Who?"

"His attorney, Jessica Pierson."

"Why do you think she's competition?"

"She's in love with him. I saw it in her eyes the day Cavan and I married. And she knows why Cavan married me."

"But you *are* married to him. Not this Jessica Pierson. There's nothing she can do about it."

"She's beautiful."

"So are you."

Meggie smiled at her sister. "Wait until you see her. But it's more than that. She and Cavan have a lot in common. She has one of those glamorous careers that men admire."

"As opposed to being a garden variety schoolteacher?"

"Exactly. And she can help Cavan with his business, which I can't. I don't even know what business he's in. He doesn't really talk to me."

"He will. Give him time."

"But you see, Caroline, he already talks to her. They've known each other a long time. She understands him. And while I know in my heart that he and I belong together, I don't really understand him."

"Do you think they've been lovers?"

Meggie nodded.

"You seem awfully calm about that."

Meggie turned her head and rested her cheek on her hand. "I am, strangely. That's in the past. Cavan has a lot of integrity and I honestly don't believe he'd take another woman as his lover as long as he's married to me."

Caroline sighed. "I wish I could find a man I trusted like that. Tom, unfortunately, was a lot like his father."

"Have you met anyone since Tom died who means anything to you?"

A slow smile curved Caroline's mouth. "One. His name is Jim James."

"Jim James?" Meggie asked with laughter in her voice.

"I know. But what his parents lacked in imagination, Jim more than makes up for. He's...delicious." Caroline grew really animated. "He's handsome, funny, charming...there are only a few things I'd like to change about him."

"So why aren't you married to him?"

"Because he hasn't asked."

"When are you going to see him again?"

"As soon as I get back to London."

"Which is when?"

"A week or so. I want to keep Grandfather company for a little longer. Besides the fact that he's not thrilled about your marriage, his textile company is in big trouble."

"That's been going on for a while."

"Then you know more than I did. He hasn't said a word to me. What I know I learned from eavesdropping. Shameful, I know, but—" she shrugged her shoulders ''—you do what you have to. He's been spending a lot of time in the north trying to get things straightened out. Oh! That reminds me—though I don't know why it reminds me. Grandfather has absolutely nothing to do with this. I'm having a dinner party when I get back to London and I want you and Cavan to come. It's something of a celebration after a year of mourning.''

"That's nice. You deserve it, but that's kind of a long way to come for a meal."

Caroline playfully pushed Meggie's shoulder. "So stay overnight and have breakfast, too."

"I'll talk to Cavan about it. Will we get to meet your Jim James?"

"If I have anything to say about it you will."

"Then we'll definitely be there."

"It's going to be black tie, so buy something completely devastating."

"In Kilgarrin?"

"That is a bit of a stretch," Caroline admitted. "Maybe Bridgit could make you something."

"Whatever. Don't worry. Your country sister won't embarrass you."

"I almost wish you would. At this point I don't know if I can stand the competition." She looked at her watch. "We'd better be getting back. I'm having dinner with Sean tonight."

"Have you seen much of him since you got here?"

"Not really. He's been caught up in becoming the best horse breeder in all of Ireland."

"Isn't that nice?" Meggie asked with a smile. "A man with a purpose."

"Hugh is furious."

"Why?"

"When was the last time you knew a Farrell to work for a living? He considers this stable job Cavan has given Sean as the supreme insult."

"That's ridiculous."

"You know it and I know it, but Hugh isn't always rational. I think all of his years of drinking too much are starting to take their toll. If I were Cavan, I wouldn't turn my back on him. Not for a minute. Hugh is blaming Cavan for everything that's ever gone wrong in his life. I don't think he has any idea how crazy he comes across to the people listening to him."

"That sounds ominous."

"I just call them as I see them." Caroline looked at her watch. "I suppose we should be going. I'm meeting Sean in less than an hour."

"I'm really glad. I think he misses his brother a lot more than he lets on."

"I do, too," Caroline said quietly. "Sometimes I try to think about how it would be if I suddenly didn't have you anymore, Meggie, and I feel so sad for him."

Meggie smiled softly as she hugged her sister. "I love you, too, Caroline. I'm glad you're home."

Chapter Seven

Meggie was busy all of the next day and arrived home on the run just as the sun was setting. As she opened the front door and stepped hurriedly inside, she walked right into Cavan's solid body. He reached out and caught her shoulders to steady her.

Without even thinking, Meggie threw her arms around his neck.

Cavan closed his eyes for a moment as his arms closed around her and held her close. He'd been away from her one day and it felt like a month.

"Am I late for our dinner?" she asked as she pulled away a little and looked up at him.

"This is one dinner it's impossible to be late for," he said as he kissed the tip of her charming nose.

"Where are we going?"

"Someplace you'll like."

"That sounds mysterious."

"Do you like mysteries?"

"I married you, didn't I?"

A slow smile curved his mouth, making her pulse soar. "So you did, Meghan." His hands fell to his sides. "You'd better change into something warmer than what you have on."

"Warmer?" She looked down at her dress and the light jacket she wore over it.

"Don't wear anything fancy. Just something comfortable and warm. We're eating out—and I do mean out."

She started up the stairs, but turned when she reached the top. "Warm and comfortable?"

He nodded, and Meggie shrugged and went to her room to go through her closets. She ended up wearing soft wool slacks and a heavy-knit sweater. Hardly stopping to look at herself in the mirror, she ran back downstairs and found Cavan waiting.

His eyes roamed over her with devastating thoroughness. "Ready?"

"Ready."

Hand in hand they walked to his car. He wordlessly held the door for her and then got in himself and headed down the long driveway. They drove for ten minutes, seemingly into the middle of nowhere, then he left the so-called main road and bumped down a dirt track for a few miles, stopping about fifty feet from where a single light glowed out of nothingness. "Where are we?" Meggie asked as Cavan opened the door for her and helped her out.

"The restaurant."

She followed him curiously, finding it hard to see. The moon and stars were out in full, but their glow was diffused by the cool, light mist that was so much a part of Ireland. What she finally saw was a wide blanket with a picnic basket on it and a kerosene lantern on the grass next to it.

As they knelt on the blanket, Cavan began unloading the basket of plates of food, a bottle of wine and two glasses. He poured them each some wine, then lifted his glass to Meggie. "Here's to an interesting evening."

Meggie lifted hers as well before drinking. She held the ruby liquid in her mouth for a moment before swallowing, enjoying its richness. "What made you think of this?" she asked in quiet delight.

"I promised you dinner out, but I didn't feel like sharing you with a roomful of people."

Cavan saw her smile in the flickering lantern light. "I love this. I can't think of anywhere I'd rather be."

"And I can't think of anyone I'd rather be with," Cavan said quietly.

The way he said the words made her heart beat faster.

"Are you hungry?"

"Not right now."

Cavan stretched his long legs out and leaned back on an elbow. "I'll have to bring you back here when it's light outside. It's beautiful."

"I can imagine."

"That's why I bought it."

"You own this?"

"It was an impulse purchase."

"You don't strike me as being at all impulsive."

"I'm not, usually. But there was something about this particular view that drew me. There's such peace here."

"More here than in America?"

He thought for a moment. "A different kind." His eyes rested on her lovely face. "And you're here."

Meggie felt suddenly shy, but she didn't drop her eyes from his shadowed face. "That makes a difference to you?"

"It's beginning to."

Now her gaze fell, so that Cavan wouldn't see the rush of joy she felt, and a comfortable silence fell between them.

Kilgarrin was a very quiet place, particularly at night. There were no factory noises as there were in some of the northern counties, and almost no traffic. Even the insects kept their noise to a minimum this night. And Cavan was at peace. In the time she'd known him, she'd never felt such a sense of complete relaxation coming from him.

"You're not as angry as you used to be, are you?" she asked.

He shook his head. "No. Which amazes me. I've been angry for ten years, but it seems to have fed on itself recently until there's very little left."

"I'm glad. Now maybe there's more room in your life for me."

"Meghan?"

"Umm?"

"Put your wine down and come here."

Her heart grew absolutely still as she set the glass on the ground and moved nearer to Cavan. He reached up and gently pulled her onto her back on the blanket, then lay on his side looking down at her. "Do you have any idea how lovely you are?"

"I hope that was rhetorical because I haven't the faintest notion of how to answer."

Again, a slow smile curved his mouth. His fingers pushed her auburn hair away from her face and onto the blanket, tangling in its silky heaviness. With devastating deliberateness, he exposed her ear and gently nuzzled her behind it. "Think of what the people in a restaurant would be whispering about us right now if they could see."

Meggie's lips parted softly as she closed her eyes, reveling in the physical sensations he could arouse in her with the lightest of touches.

Cavan raised his head and gazed down at her as his hand lightly caressed her throat. "There are so many things you don't know about me."

Meggie slowly opened her eyes. "I know all I need to."

"You have no idea of the kind of man I am, or the things I've done to get where I am."

Meggie gazed at him with eyes full of tenderness and love. "I may not know what you've done, but I think I know even better than you what kind of man you are."

"You're not really seeing me. You're seeing a man you created from your romantic imagination."

Meggie shook her head. "Let me tell you about yourself. When you were younger, you enjoyed life.

You trusted people. You were capable of loving. You had ambitions for your future. But the people you trusted and loved—such as my sister—betrayed you. You were hurt in one of the worst ways imaginable, and you began focusing all of your ambitions on hurting those who had hurt you. That doesn't make you an evil person. It only makes you human."

"It's not that cut and dried, Meghan."

"Of course it isn't. I'm just telling you what I see when I look at you. When I look at my husband."

Cavan lay on his back and pulled Meggie close to his side, his strong arm around her shoulders. "When did Caroline tell you about us?"

"Yesterday." Meggie nestled her head under his chin. "She thought it would be better coming from her."

"I suppose."

"I can't imagine choosing Tom Farrell over you."

She felt him smile in the darkness. "You'd make a good diplomat." He exhaled a long, deep breath. "You understand, don't you, that there's nothing between Caroline and me now?"

Meggie nodded under his chin.

"What a mistake that would have been. We would have made each other miserable."

Meggie raised up and looked down at Cavan. "I'm glad."

Cavan lifted a dark brow.

"Oh! Not glad that you would have been miserable, but that you don't have any lingering feelings for my sister."

He grew serious as he gazed at her lovely face. "You're so different from anyone I've ever known before. You've given me your heart without my asking for it, and without any guarantees of my ever giving you mine. Not many people have that kind of courage."

"Some would call it a courageous stupidity."

"What would you call it?"

She rested her cheek on his chest and toyed with a button on his shirt. "I don't have a name for it, but I remember a quote by Anna Dickinson I came across about a year after we met. I've never forgotten it. 'There are souls that are created for one another in the eternities, hearts that are predestined each to each, from the absolute necessities of their nature; and when this man and woman come face to face, their hearts throb and are one.' That's how I felt the day I met you. The difference between us is that it's taking you a little longer to realize it. I mean, you haven't yet, have you?" she asked hopefully.

Cavan's arm tightened around her as he buried his face in her hair. "I need more time, Meghan. I wasn't ready for anyone like you to come into my life. It takes a lot of adjusting. Living with you as your husband is going to take a lot of adjusting."

"Why?"

There was a short silence. "Do you know how I've gotten the money I have? Gambling. That's what I've done for years, all over the world. And I've been lucky. What I won, I invested, and those investments turned out to be good ones. I've never really had one place—aside from prison—that I could call home. Or

one woman I wanted to be just mine. And I never felt
any particular void.''

"Admit it. You'd miss me if I wasn't here.''

Cavan shifted, rolling Meggie gently back onto the
blanket, and looked down at her. "I would.''

"You don't sound happy about that.''

"I don't like being dependent on anyone else for
anything.''

Meggie raised her arms and tangled her fingers in his
thick hair. "Almost anything,'' she murmured as she
pulled his mouth to hers.

His tongue slowly and suggestively explored every
corner of her mouth, learning the sweet taste of her
and making it his.

When his mouth left hers to caress the clean line of
her jaw, Meggie tilted her head back, exposing her
long throat. "Oh,'' she sighed as a subtle warmth
filled her abdomen, "you do that well.''

"I do a lot of things well.''

"Cavan...''

"Shh.'' His hand slid under her sweater and softly
rubbed her smooth skin as his mouth moved back to
hers. The kiss grew deeper as his hand moved to her
softly rounded breast, bare under the sweater.

Meggie inhaled sharply and then moaned against his
mouth as the warmth that had gathered in her abdomen began to spread. She could feel Cavan's desire
hard against her thigh, intensifying her own.

Her own hands moved down his back, pulling his
shirt out from his pants and then running her fingertips up over his smoothly muscled back.

"We shouldn't be doing this," he whispered next to her ear just before kissing it.

"We're married."

She felt him shake his head just before he rolled off of her. "Technically."

Meggie caught her lower lip between her teeth. "Is it me? Is it that you're not attracted to me?"

Cavan sat up and pulled Meggie into a sitting position. He tenderly tucked her hair behind her ears and then cupped her face in his hands. "The problem is that I'm very attracted to you. I've never not wanted to sleep with you. But I'm not sure I'm in love with you."

"Is that a prerequisite?"

"It is with you. I don't want to make any mistakes. It has to be right for both of us or it won't be right at all. You aren't the kind of woman a man has sex with. You're the kind of woman a man makes love to." He pulled her toward him and rested his mouth against her forehead. "Do you understand?"

She nodded.

"Good. Now let's have some dinner."

Meggie moved away from him and took a shaky breath. "I don't think I'm very hungry."

"Then think about Millie's reaction when we bring back all of this food untouched."

A smile touched Meggie's mouth. "Maybe I could eat a little something."

"Good girl." He handed her some soda bread smothered in fresh butter. "More wine?"

"No, thank you."

"Did anything interesting happen while I was gone?" He was trying hard to make them both forget what had just passed between the two of them.

"Not really. Sarah's all better. Oh, but there is one thing. I'd like to invite you to a ball the orphanage is giving this weekend."

"A ball at an orphanage? That's a little unusual, isn't it?"

"Not really. They have one every year to raise funds. The children do all of the planning and decorating themselves. People in the community donate the refreshments and music."

"That sounds nice."

"It's lovely. Will you go with me?"

"I'd like that, thank you."

Meggie smiled at him. "Good. Then it's a date."

She finished the bread and wiped her fingers on an napkin that Cavan handed her.

"Would you like anything else?"

"No. I'm a little tired, though. I think I'd like to go home now."

"All right." She helped him repack the basket and fold the blanket. They used the lantern to show them the way to the car.

The drive back was a quiet one, each lost in their own thoughts. Meggie was unaware of the blue eyes that rested on her profile from time to time until she turned her head and found her gaze locked with his. Suddenly Cavan reached out and covered her hand with his. Meggie turned hers over and wound her fingers through his.

Long after Cavan turned his attention back to the road, Meggie stared. Cavan had a very clean profile, but that wasn't what she saw. She saw a man she loved more than life, and for the first time she had to admit to herself that he might never love her the same way.

She swallowed hard and turned her head so that he wouldn't see the tears she had to blink back. Meggie O'Neill, the eternal optimist, didn't know if she'd be able to go on without him, and it frightened her.

When Cavan parked in front of the house he turned to talk to Meggie, but she got quickly out of the car. The last thing she wanted was for him to see how upset she was.

Cavan followed her up the steps, a curious frown creasing his brow. He stepped into the foyer behind her and stood perfectly still for a moment, then looked toward the living room.

"What's wrong?" Meggie asked, her eyes following the same path as his and seeing nothing.

"Jessica is here."

"How do you know?"

"Her perfume."

Meggie hated it that he knew her perfume so well. Sure enough, she walked into view a moment later, looking lovely and smiling a greeting. "Cavan, how are you?" When she looked at Meggie she was still smiling, but she grew considerably cooler. "The housekeeper told me you were out to dinner." She glanced down at the picnic basket Cavan held.

"What are you doing here, Jessica? I thought you were in New York until Thursday."

"I was, but something came up that I needed to talk to you about."

"Couldn't you have called?"

Meggie was happy to see that Cavan wasn't particularly pleased to see his lovely attorney.

"I chose not to. I thought it was too important to trust to a telephone."

Cavan sighed and turned to Meggie. "I'm sorry. Would you excuse us, Meghan?"

"Certainly," she said quietly. "I'm rather tired anyway. I'll see you in the morning." She started to turn away, but Cavan caught her arm and turned her back to face him.

"Are you all right?"

She nodded, not meeting his gaze.

Cavan raised her face to his, forcing her to look at him. "Are you sure?"

"As I said, I'm a little tired."

His thumb gently rubbed her cheek where a tear had traced its way down. "So I see. Good night, Meghan."

She looked at him for a long, silent moment. "Good night, Cavan." Then she looked at the woman standing behind him. "Will you be spending the night here, Jessica?"

"No. I have a room at the Kilgarrin Inn."

"I see. Well, good night, then."

She felt Cavan's eyes on her as she walked up the stairs, but didn't turn back. When she got to her room, she slipped into a simple nightgown and climbed into bed, all without turning on the lights. She hadn't lied about being tired, yet she couldn't sleep.

It was obvious that Jessica was still in love with Cavan. How could she compete with someone like that? Jessica was a sophisticated, highly professional woman.

But there was a lot more to the way Meggie was feeling than the presence of Jessica Pierson.

A kind of cloud had settled over Meggie on the way back from the picnic. She couldn't rid herself of the feeling that something disastrous was going to happen. She had no idea what it was; only that it was indeed inevitable.

It was the same kind of feeling she'd had just before her parents had died.

Meggie sighed into the darkness and rolled onto her side, hugging her pillow against her. For the first time in years, Meggie wasn't looking forward to tomorrow.

But it was going to come whether she wanted it to or not. She turned restlessly onto her back and stared at the ceiling for more than an hour, her thoughts flitting here and there with no direction. She finally gave up and turned on the bedside lamp, then rose and paced her room.

The man standing outside leaning against a tree as he smoked a cigarette watched her silhouette passing back and forth as her shadow was cast on the drawn bedroom shade.

His thoughts echoed hers.

Something was going to happen. Even he felt it in the air.

Chapter Eight

When Meggie came downstairs the next morning, Millie met her coming up the steps. "There you are. I thought I was going to have to wake you." She looked at her closely. "Are you all right?"

"Just tired. Would you get me some coffee, Millie? That's all I have time for before I leave for school."

"Certainly. I'll get it right away. But first, your husband wanted me to tell you that he had to leave early this morning, and he won't be back for the rest of the week."

"Did he say why?"

"No."

"Was Jessica with him?"

"That one," Millie said disparagingly. "She was."

Meggie's heart sank, despite the fact that she knew Cavan wouldn't do anything with Jessica while he was married.

Someone knocked on the door and Meggie started toward it while Millie headed for the kitchen. Sean stood there. "Morning!" he said cheerfully as he walked past her into the house.

"Good morning. Please, feel free to come in."

He turned and grinned at her, but then his grin faded. "You look awful."

She closed the door. "Thank you for helping me start the day on such an up note."

"Sorry, but you do. Is something wrong?"

"No. What brings you here so early?"

"I wanted to talk to Cavan about that beautiful attorney of his."

"Jessica," Meggie sighed in resignation. "What about her?"

"I want to know what kind of flowers she likes."

Meggie lifted an expressive brow. "Why?"

"Because I want to send her dozens of them."

"Good. I hope you sweep her off her feet."

"I think I already have. I stopped by to talk to Cavan last night about the horses, but you and he were out to dinner."

"And Jessica was here."

"And how. We had a long talk. I invited her to the orphanage ball and she accepted."

"She didn't," Meggie groaned.

"She did."

Meggie knew exactly why Jessica had accepted. She figured that Cavan would be there. But she didn't say that to Sean. "I'm happy for you. I'm sure you'll have a lovely time."

"I intend to." He looked at her more closely. "Are you sure you're all right?"

"Stop asking me that. I don't know why I can't have the occasional bad night like everyone else without being asked if I'm all right fourteen times in the course of a morning."

"I'm sorry."

Meggie tiredly rubbed her forehead. "No, Sean, you haven't anything to be sorry about. I'm the one who should be apologizing for taking my bad humor out on an innocent bystander."

"Want to talk about it?"

She shook her head. "It wouldn't help. Oh, thank you," she smiled at Millie as the housekeeper handed her a cup of hot, black coffee.

Sean waited until the housekeeper had gone. "Can I be straight with you, Meggie?"

"You usually are."

"If you ever need someone, I'm here for you."

"I know that."

"I should have married you."

Meggie looked at him curiously. "What are you talking about? We both decided it would be wrong."

"That was before I realized I was in love with you."

Suddenly Meggie flashed him a smile. "That was only after you knew you couldn't have me."

"So?"

"So that's not love. That's the old grass is always greener syndrome. I think Jessica proves that point rather nicely, don't you?" she asked as she took another sip of coffee.

Sean smiled as well. "God, I'm shallow."

"If you think I'm going to argue the point with you, forget it." She kissed his cheek. "But I love you anyway." She looked at her watch. "Oh, dear. I'm going to be late. May I borrow your car again? I promise to get one of my own soon."

"What are you talking about? Isn't that your car outside?"

"What car?"

Sean opened the door while Meggie set down her cup and followed him. At the foot of the stairs was a brand-new red sports car, just like the one that had burned. Meggie ran down to it and opened the driver's door. A big bow was attached to the steering wheel and a card was on the dash. She opened it and smiled at the note scrawled in Cavan's legible hand. "Happy Birthday a month early."

"Oh," she said softly as she hugged the card to her breast. "You shouldn't have."

"I didn't," Sean said from over her shoulder.

"Not you."

"But I would have if I'd had the money."

"Thank you for the thought."

"You're welcome."

"Is there anything else you'd like to say?"

Sean thought for a moment. "Can't think of a thing."

"Then I'm going to school. I'll see you later. Caroline is probably coming over for dinner. Would you like to join us?"

"Sure. Thanks."

He closed the door after her and stood back as she started the engine and raced it a little, then watched as she drove off. "Cavan," he said to the air, "you're a fool if you don't know what a gem you have in her."

Meggie stood in front of her full-length mirror and stared at herself. The ball gown she wore was emerald-green silk over several full petticoats. The top was square cut with two thin straps over her shapely shoulders. She had braided her auburn hair earlier when it was damp, and then taken the braids out and combed it, leaving it fashionably kinked. She brushed one side up over her ear and held it in place with a gold comb. Two long gold earrings hung from her earlobes.

There was a knock on her door and Meggie, smiling, ran to answer it. "Cavan!"

Millie looked at her apologetically. "Sorry, dear, but it's just me. I still haven't heard anything from him. Are you sure you told him what night the ball was?"

"I'm sure. I guess he just forgot."

"Well that Jessica Pierson woman made it back in time. Sean's already left to pick her up."

"Speaking of which, I should be going if I don't want to be late." Meggie tried to sound as though it didn't bother her that Cavan wasn't there, but Millie read through it. Men. They were more trouble than they could ever be worth.

"You stay late and have a good time."

"I will. Don't wait up."

Meggie went back to her bed and picked up a wrap that matched her dress, flinging one end of it casually over her shoulder, then going outside to her car. She sat behind the steering wheel for a moment before finally starting the engine and driving off.

Millie stood in the doorway, waving her off with a smile, but muttering under her breath. When that man came home, she was going to have a few things to say to him, whether he wanted to hear them or not.

Meggie took the safe way to the orphanage. As she approached it, she had to smile. Lights shone from nearly every window. Lanterns hung in the gardens, sparkling brightly in the night. She was a little late and had to park on the grass. Cars behind her followed suit. There was an outer door that led directly into the castle ballroom and Meggie followed the lighted path to it, her steps matching the soft rhythm of the music that drifted around her.

When she walked through the double doors, there was a receiving line with Father Flaherty at its head and some of the nuns who ran the orphanage, and then the children themselves—at least the ones who were old enough to be up this late.

Father Flaherty took both of her hands in his and gazed at her with shining eyes. "My, you look like a picture. Where's your husband?"

"He got held up on business."

"That's too bad, but perhaps I can take up some of the slack on your dancing card."

She just smiled at him, and went on through the line, then chatted with people she knew as she made her way through the beautifully decorated ballroom.

Flowers were everywhere, picked fresh from the gardens. Their scent hung lightly in the air. The music was elegant and eminently danceable, if one had someone to dance with. She saw Sean with Jessica and tried her best not to be too close to them. She would have loved to have been able to ask Jessica about Cavan but it seemed degrading not to know where her own husband was.

"Meggie!"

She turned to find her sister hurrying across the room toward her, a handsome, brown-haired, brown-eyed man in tow.

"Sorry we're late, but Jim didn't get to Kilgarrin until an hour ago, and then he had to change, and..." She raised her hand. "Well, it's a long story." She turned to the man with her. "Jim James, I'd like you to meet my sister, Meggie Gallagher."

Meggie held out her hand and smiled. "I've been looking forward to meeting you."

"Where's Cavan?" Caroline's eyes circled the room.

"Not here. He couldn't make it. I haven't seen Grandfather, either. Where is he?"

"In the north."

"The company?"

"Isn't it always lately?"

The music started after a brief pause, and Jim smiled down at Caroline, then at Meggie. "Would you feel deserted if we took to the floor? I haven't seen your sister in weeks and I've missed her."

It warmed Meggie's heart to watch them. "Envious, perhaps, but not deserted."

He winked at her and pulled Caroline into his arms.

"May I have the pleasure?"

She turned to find Father Flaherty beside her, his arm gallantly extended. "I'd love to, thank you."

He swung her into the dance with the energy of a man half his age.

"How is the fund-raising going?"

"We've outdone ourselves this year," he beamed. "Every year we get a few more people here, and every year we get a little more money. I wish we could have two of these a year, but I'm afraid that might be overkill."

"It's hard to believe that this one's almost over."

"Yes. Just half an hour more. And then I'm going to go home and sleep for a week. I'm getting too old for this."

"Never."

"I'd like to hear you say that when you turn seventy." Then his amused tone was replaced by one more serious. "Hugh Farrell has been looking at you strangely this evening."

"Hugh? I didn't even know he was here."

"Arrived alone about an hour ago. He hasn't taken to the dance floor yet, but then he probably doesn't feel much like dancing these days."

"I can imagine."

"Still, I don't like the way he's looking at you. There's something real odd about it."

Suddenly Meggie's eyes fastened on something over Father Flaherty's shoulder and she stumbled. He stopped dancing and turned to see what she was looking at.

Cavan stood in the doorway dressed in a black tuxedo. His eyes never left Meggie as he made his way across the room to her. "Excuse me, Father, but I'd like to finish this dance with my wife."

With a wordless flourish, he turned Meggie over to her husband and walked away, smiling.

As Cavan put his hand at Meggie's waist and took her hand in his, he felt her tremble, and pulled her a little closer. "Sorry I'm late, Meghan."

"It's all right. You came." Her eyes were filled with so much love that Cavan wanted to take her off somewhere where they could be alone, but he settled for holding her closer as they danced.

"I missed you."

She smiled up at him. "Good."

"Let's go home."

"But you just got here."

"Does it matter?" His hand moved gently on her back, pressing her hips more tightly to his as they moved in rhythm to the slowly pulsing music.

Meggie felt a rush that left her breathless. "No, I guess not."

Neither of them noticed the menacing eyes of Hugh
Farrell watching their every move, so wrapped up were
they in each other.

"I love you, Meghan."

She stopped dancing and stood staring at him, her
lips softly parted.

Cavan ached to pull her into his arms, but as he
looked around the ballroom, he saw that they were
beginning to attract a smiling audience. "Come on."
He grabbed her hand and pulled her along behind
him, out of the orphanage and into the parking lot.
Without a word he helped her into his car and drove
home, then parked the car and raced with her up the
steps and into the house.

Still in the foyer, he pulled her into his arms and
gazed down at her. "I do love you. I don't know why
it took me so long to figure it out. I only know that I
don't ever want to be away from you again."

His mouth came down on hers with a hunger that
matched her own.

"Oh, dear."

Meggie and Cavan, still in each other's arms, turned
toward the voice at the top of the stairs. "I'm sorry to
interrupt," Millie said, "but you had an urgent call a
little while ago, Cavan."

"I'll return it tomorrow."

"I'm afraid the gentleman said he needed to speak
with you tonight."

"Did he leave a name?"

"Johnson. Robert Johnson, from America."

Cavan looked down at Meggie with a wry smile and then kissed her forehead. "Hold that thought. I'll meet you in the bedroom."

Meggie wrapped her arms around his neck and pulled his mouth to hers. "You hold that thought," she said softly, and then climbed the stairs.

Cavan watched her all the way up, then went into the library to make the call.

Meggie went to her room and slipped out of her dress and into her favorite nightgown. It was a pale-pink crisp cotton with yards of material, and lace at her neck and at the waist-high slits up the sides. It was so full that the slits couldn't be seen unless she was walking.

Meggie sat on the edge of the bed and brushed her hair in long strokes, then turned out the overhead light and turned on the small lamp on the bedside table before climbing under the covers to wait for Cavan.

And to think it was only a week ago that she'd had such ominous feelings about the future. How wonderful to find she'd been wrong. Nothing had happened. Cavan was here. He was fine.

She smiled. He was in love with her.

As she lay there thinking, her eyelids grew heavier and heavier. What was taking him so long?

By the time Cavan knocked, Meggie was sound asleep. He opened the door and walked over to the bed to look down at her. A tender smile that would have surprised those who knew Cavan curved his mouth as he sat on the edge of the bed and watched her sleep.

"Meghan?" he whispered.

She moved, but she didn't wake.

"Meghan?" he whispered again, stroking the hair away from her forehead.

She slowly opened her eyes and smiled sleepily. "Hello at last."

Cavan leaned over and kissed her deeply, then looked down at her again. "I'm sorry, Meghan, but I have to go."

Meggie raised up on her elbows. "Where? Why?"

"To New York. I'm trying to unload one of the businesses I bought, and there are some complications. I'll tell you exactly what it is when I come back."

"Is Jessica going with you?"

"Would it bother you if she were?"

Meggie shook her head. "Not anymore."

"Good. It shouldn't. As it is, though, I haven't been able to get in touch with her. I left a message where she's staying to catch the next plane." He looked at his watch. "Which is exactly what I should be doing right now."

Hazel eyes gazed into blue. "Can't you stay just a little longer?"

Cavan trailed his fingers down her cheek. "A little longer won't do it, Meghan. When we make love for the first time, it's going to take all night, not a few hurried minutes."

He pressed her back against the pillow and kissed her, then slowly trailed his mouth down her body, lightly brushing it across each of her breasts through the cotton. "I'll be back early tomorrow," he said softly as he kissed her again, then turned off the bedside lamp and left.

Meggie sighed deeply as she lay there. She heard him in his room and then a moment later the front door slammed shut. A car started and then drove away.

Meggie put her hands over the breasts his lips had so recently touched and closed her eyes.

Tomorrow.

Chapter Nine

There was no school the next day, so Meggie spent her time alternately pacing through the house and riding her horse. As she walked into the house after riding, Millie was waiting for her. "Oh, Meggie, I'm so glad you're here. That Jessica Pierson woman showed up and I didn't know what to do with her so I put her in the library."

"Did you tell her where Cavan was?"

"I did, but she said it didn't matter because she was here to see you, not him. What do you suppose she wants?"

"I have a pretty good idea." She glanced into a mirror and brushed her hair by running her fingers through it in long strokes. "How do I look?"

"Like you lost your comb."

"Thank you, Millie," she said dryly.

The housekeeper just smiled. "I made tea for her and served it in the library. Would you like me to bring you a cup?"

"I don't think so, thanks anyway. I don't expect she's here to be sociable." Meggie took a deep breath and straightened her shoulders, feeling a little as though she were throwing herself up to the lions. "On second thought, I would like some, Millie." Then she walked into the library.

Jessica sat comfortably on the couch reading a magazine. Meggie closed the door behind her and sat on the arm of the couch across from her. "My housekeeper said you wished to see me."

Her blue eyes looked Meggie over very thoroughly. "I'm glad to see she can relay accurate messages."

"I'll pass the compliment along. And speaking of messages, did you get Cavan's? He said he left one where you were staying that you were to meet him in New York."

"I got the message, but I feel that this is more important right now."

Meggie nodded. "I see. So, Jessica, what can I do for you?"

"I want Cavan back."

"I wasn't aware that I had taken him from you."

"You aren't aware of a lot of things."

"Such as?"

She hesitated just long enough for Meggie to realize that this was difficult for her, and as a result Meggie's own attitude toward Jessica changed to one of sympathy rather than hostility. Jessica rose from the couch and walked to the window to stare outside. "I'm in love with him. I've been in love with him for years."

"Believe me when I say that I'm entirely empathetic with that, Jessica."

"You, too?"

"Me, too."

"But you see, you had a chance to do something about it. I never did. Ever since he got out of prison, his entire existence has been dedicated to making money and ruining the people who put him there. To this day, I don't think he ever really looked at me. I mean, we slept together, but it didn't mean anything to him. At first it didn't mean anything to me, either."

"But later that changed?"

Jessica nodded. "And when it did, he shut me out of his life. His personal life, at least. I talked him into keeping me as his attorney."

"That must have hurt."

"It did, even though I know he didn't do it to be cruel, but to keep me from getting hurt. He wasn't capable of loving anybody and he knew it. Over the last five years, whenever any woman has started getting serious about him, he's turned away."

Meggie said nothing.

"Even when he married you, it was with that same single-minded purpose." She turned to face Meggie. "But you were different. He felt things for you."

Still Meggie said nothing when she paused.

"I want you to get an annulment."

Meggie looked at her in amazement. "No. I can't believe you'd even ask that."

"A marriage born in hatred can never survive. Give it up now before you get any more deeply involved."

Meggie rose from the arm of the couch. "I think you've just overstayed your welcome in my house, Jessica."

"I didn't want to do this, Meggie, but you're forcing me. There's something in all of this no one has bothered to tell you. I suppose it's some effort at misguided protection. You think the reason Cavan married you was to keep your money and your lineage out of the Farrell family, don't you?"

"That's right."

"Well, that makes it all nice and neat, doesn't it? Nothing personal against you or your family."

Meggie thought she saw where all of this was headed. "If you're going to tell me that he was trying to get back at my sister, you're wrong. Cavan and I have talked about that."

"No, Meggie. I wasn't going to tell you that. His real reason was to strike a blow at a man who played a very large part in sending him to prison."

"Hugh Farrell."

Jessica shook her head as she looked at Meggie for a long moment then said softly, "Your grandfather, Padraic O'Neill."

A cup and saucer crashed to the floor in the doorway just inside the library. Millie stooped quickly down to retrieve the broken pieces while the two women inside never broke their concentration on one another.

"What?" Meggie asked in a hoarse whisper.

Jessica watched the color drain from Meggie's face but felt no satisfaction.

"You must be wrong. You must be. My grandfather would never do anything like that."

Jessica walked back to the couch and shouldered her purse. "I'm sorry, but he did. It was the only way he could be sure Cavan wouldn't be around to bother your sister again."

Meggie felt physically ill. "But to send him to prison..." She just stood there, remembering the clashes between Cavan and her grandfather. Remembering some of the things her grandfather had said that hadn't made any sense at the time, but which made perfect sense now that she knew what had happened. Meggie put her fingers over her mouth as she looked at Jessica. "This can't be true."

"Whether Cavan recognizes it or not at the moment, you'll always be an O'Neill to him. There are times when he'll look at you and see your grandfather. There will be times when he hates you. He'll never be able to love you without qualification. And if you need proof that Cavan still hates Padraic O'Neill, ask him about AmeriTextiles. That's one of Cavan's companies." She walked toward the library door. "I'll see myself out."

Meggie ran her fingers distractedly through her hair. Her grandfather. She had to talk to her grandfather. Literally running out of the house and across the lawn to the coach house, she banged on Sean's door again and again, but he didn't answer. "Sean!" she yelled. "I need to borrow your car again. I left mine at the orphanage last night."

There was no reply, and now that she looked around, she saw that his car was gone.

Meggie hit the door in frustration with her balled up fist and then ran to the stables where she saddled a horse and galloped down the drive and onto the public road toward her grandfather's house. When she got there fifteen minutes later, both she and the horse were winded. She jumped from the horse and raced up the steps and into the house where she'd spent most of her life. "Grandfather!"

She ran to the library and opened the double doors, but he wasn't there. "Grandfather!" she called again.

Caroline came down the steps and looked at her sister as though she'd lost her mind. "What on earth are you screaming about?"

Meggie took several deep breaths. "I need to speak with Grandfather."

"He's here somewhere. Calm down."

"Please, Caroline, I need to talk to him now. Find him for me. I'll be waiting in the library."

Caroline responded to the urgency in Meggie's voice and went through the house looking for their grandfather.

Meggie paced back and forth in the library, waiting. When her grandfather finally came, he stood in the doorway watching her until she saw him. Then she stopped pacing and just stared at him. He closed the doors behind him on a curious Caroline, and moved toward Meggie. When he tried to touch her, she recoiled.

"You know, don't you?" he asked.

Meggie just looked at him. "Why didn't you tell me when Cavan first showed up with the contract? You knew it was more complicated than I thought it was. More horrible."

"I couldn't," he said quietly. "I didn't want to ever see the look in your eyes that's there now. Did Cavan tell you?"

"No. He doesn't even know that I know."

A long silence fell between them until Meggie broke it with a one-word question. "Why?"

"Why did I do it?" He shook his head. "I had reasons that at the time were very good ones. I never mean to hurt anyone, but nothing I do now can ever make up for it."

"Cavan lost five years of his life."

Her grandfather said nothing.

"Five years." Her hazel eyes were dark with pain. "I feel as though someone I've loved all my life has just died," she said quietly as she walked past him and out the door.

Caroline was still waiting in the hall. "Meggie, are you all—"

But Meggie was already out the door.

"—right?"

Meggie crashed headlong into Cavan. He caught her in his arms. "Meggie, I just talked to Millie. She told me what Jessica said."

"Let go of me."

"Not until you hear me out."

"I don't want to hear anything you or my grandfather have to say. You've both lied to me until I can't trust either of you anymore. Let me go."

She struggled so hard that Cavan was afraid she'd hurt herself so he released her shoulders, and Meggie ran past him to her horse and took off across the estate. He started to chase her in his car but there were fences in the way so he pulled in front of the stables and followed her on one of her grandfather's horses.

She had so much of a head start that he knew the only way he'd catch her was if she slowed down or stopped, and he didn't think there was much likelihood of that. The best he could do was to keep her in sight as they rode.

Meggie crossed the property line dividing her grandfather's land from Cavan's, taking the same path she'd used almost every day of her life in Ireland.

Suddenly a loud crack split the air and almost simultaneously something stung her shoulder with enough force to knock her from her horse. She fell to the ground hard. The back of her head hit a rock on the side of the path, and Meggie knew no more.

Cavan heard the shot, and watched in helpless horror as Meggie flew through the air. He raced his horse even harder, but everything seemed to be moving in slow motion. This was like some nightmare. When he was finally there, he jumped off the still running horse.

When he got to Meggie, he stood for a moment looking down at her. She was so still. He bent over her, afraid to touch her. "Meggie?"

She didn't answer.

His throat closed. "Meggie, please say something."

He pressed his fingertips to the vulnerable spot at the base of her throat and found a soft pulse.

He breathed a quiet thank-you and then set about examining her more closely. Nothing looked broken, but her shoulder was bleeding profusely. He took off his shirt and ripped it into strips, then opened her blouse and bound the wound. Who would want to shoot her? And why? Meggie had no enemies.

He hated to move her, but he couldn't leave her alone while he went for help. Whoever had fired that gun might still be out there somewhere. With a gentleness of which he wouldn't have believed himself capable, Cavan started to lift her in his arms. Then he saw the rock. He looked down at her closed eyes. "Oh, Meggie," he said in a thick voice. "What have I done to you?"

He lifted her close to his heart and carried her with as little motion as possible back to her grandfather's. Caroline met him at the door. "What happened?"

"She was shot."

"Oh, my God. By whom?"

"I don't know. Get your grandfather and call a doctor. Now," he added when she hesitated. "Tell the doctor that there's also a head injury."

He carried her up the stairs to the first bedroom he came to and laid her gently on the bed, then stood gazing down at her. She was so pale and lifeless. He couldn't even see her breathing, yet he knew she was.

Padraic O'Neill came running in out of breath. "Caroline told me that Meggie was shot."

"She was. The bullet hit her in the shoulder, but it knocked her from the horse and she hit her head on a rock. The bullet is the least of our worries at the moment."

"But who would do such a thing?"

Cavan shook his head. "I don't know, but I'm sure as hell going to find out." He searched for Meggie's pulse again. "Where is that doctor?"

"He has to come from the next county."

"She should be in a hospital."

"We don't have one in Kilgarrin."

Cavan ran his fingers distractedly through his hair and walked over to the window. The old man watched the younger man's shoulders slump forward. Cavan rubbed his forehead and his eyes before he turned back into the room and pulled up a chair next to the bed. He took one of Meggie's cold hands in his and chafed it a little to give it warmth, then held it against his mouth. "Don't leave me, Meghan," he whispered. "I've just found you. Don't leave me now."

Padraic O'Neill stretched an unsteady hand to clasp Cavan's shoulder. "She'll be fine. You'll see."

Cavan just held on to Meggie's hand, afraid to take his eyes from her. Caroline came in a moment later and hovered in silence near the foot of the bed.

"Tell him, Grandfather," she said after a few minutes. "Tell Cavan what you told me earlier."

"It doesn't matter now."

"But it does."

Cavan looked up at her. "What are you talking about?"

"The only reason Grandfather helped Hugh Farrell send you to prison was because Hugh threatened Meggie's safety. She was twelve years old and away at school most of the time, but she was home for vacations. Short of locking her up, there wasn't much Grandfather could do to protect her."

"It was either you or my granddaughter, and I'm sorry, but as far as I was concerned I had no choice. If I had said or done anything to contradict his testimony, I would have lost my granddaughter."

"You really think he would have done that?"

"There's no question in my mind. He's crazy."

"And you would have let Meggie marry his son?"

"Sean isn't the problem. It's his father. And again it was the same story with the contract. Meggie's father made it, and Hugh saw to it that I would never break it."

Cavan held Meggie's hand against his cheek. "And then I came along."

"That's right. I can't blame you for the hatred you had toward me, but yet again, Meggie became the pawn. The weapon of your revenge. Either she married you or you would tell her that I lied to send you to prison, knowing that she'd never be able to forgive something like that."

"And then I started on your business."

"With remarkable results."

Cavan looked at the old man for a long moment. "I don't know if this will make you feel any better, but the reason I went back to New York last night was to finish the sale of AmeriTextiles to someone who isn't going to be willing to pour nearly the amount of cash into that business that I was to compete with you."

"What made you do that?"

He looked back at the woman on the bed. "It's very hard to fuel any kind of hatred when you love someone. You're her grandfather. If I hurt you, I hurt her, and I couldn't bear that."

The front knocker sounded through the house.

"That must be the doctor." Caroline raced out of the room to answer the door. A moment later a man in his early forties walked into the room and went straight to Meggie. "Caroline gave me a rundown on what happened, Paddy. Do you know who did it?"

"I've a fairly good idea."

Cavan looked up at him. "Farrell?"

"That's right."

"You call the police, Paddy, while I check out Meggie." The doctor looked at Cavan. "Who are you?"

"Her husband."

"Then you can stay." He got out a penlight and checked Meggie's eyes for a reaction. "That's good," he said. Then he probed the back of her head. "Has she been conscious since it happened?"

"No."

"And judging from when Caroline called, she hit her head about an hour ago."

"That's right." Cavan looked down at her still pale face. "She should be in a hospital."

"Rubbish. There isn't anything more that can be done for her in a hospital than we can do right here." He probed the back of her head. "That's quite a knot she's got there. You might put a little ice on that later to help the swelling." He leaned further over Meggie and pressed against her sternum. Meggie moaned softly, and the doctor smiled with satisfaction. "I think she'll be all right. Now let's take a look at that bullet wound. Did you see what kind of gun was used?"

"No. I just heard the shot."

The doctor removed the makeshift bandage from her shoulder and examined the wound. "Well, it must have been a small caliber. And it went all the way through. A little cleaning and we'll have that taken care of."

Meggie's grandfather came in at that moment with a sweater that he handed to Cavan. "I had Millie bring this over."

Cavan looked down at his bare torso. "I didn't even realize. Thank you."

"You've had a few other things on your mind. How is she?"

"I think she'll be all right. I'd like someone to stay with her tonight to keep an eye on her."

"I will," Cavan said as he finished slipping the sweater over his head.

"Caroline and I will help."

The doctor nodded as he finished putting the patch bandage on Meggie's shoulder. "I'm going to put her arm in a sling. I'd appreciate it if you could find some pajamas for her to wear. She's going to be in bed for a few days."

Caroline was standing in the doorway. "I'll find something for her."

"And while you're at it, put some ice in a hot-water bottle and cork it. I want that behind her head." He started packing up his things.

"That's all?" Cavan asked.

"That's all. I expect her to wake in an hour or two, but not for long. She'll probably be disoriented and go right back to sleep. If she hasn't come completely around in, say, ten hours, there may be complications, but I don't foresee any at this point. What she has is a pretty straightforward concussion. I'll be back in the morning to check on her and to change the dressing on her shoulder. Call me any time between now and then if you get worried. Any questions?"

Cavan shook his head, his eyes still on Meggie.

"I'll walk you to the door, Doctor," Paddy said. "Thank you for getting here so quickly."

Caroline squeezed past them in the doorway. "Here's a nightgown. It should fit her." She held it out to Cavan. "You put it on her while I get the ice."

Cavan sat on the bed next to Meggie and undressed her with gentle hands, then slipped the nightgown on her. "Open your eyes, Meggie," he said quietly. "Look at me."

She didn't.

He laid her back against her pillow and covered her warmly with the sheet and down comforter. Caroline came in with the ice and set it behind Meggie's head. She watched as Cavan went about laying wood in the large fireplace on the wall opposite the bed and lighting it.

"I'm surprised you didn't take off after Hugh Farrell."

It was getting dark outside and Cavan turned on a small lamp near Meggie's bed. "First Meggie. Then Farrell."

"The police won't arrest him, you know. There's no evidence. Not even a bullet."

"I'll find the bullet. He's not going to get away with this, Caroline."

"Good."

Meggie moved a little and Cavan quickly sat on the edge of the bed, her hand in his. "Meghan? Come on, Meghan."

Caroline sat on the other side of the bed. "She's so pale."

"I know."

She heard the tightness in his voice. "You really love her, don't you?"

He reached out and touched Meggie's smooth cheek. Caroline watched the muscle in his jaw work. "I don't know what I'll do if anything happens to her."

Caroline touched his arm. "You'll go on with your life. But nothing is going to happen to her."

He leaned forward and rested his lips against Meggie's forehead. "Wake up, Meghan. Wake up and smile at me. Tell me you love me. Let me tell you I love you."

Caroline rose unnoticed from the bed and left the room.

Cavan moved to the chair after a while, but his eyes never left Meggie. After a couple of hours he thought he saw her eyelids flicker. He moved back to the bed and looked down at her. "Meghan?"

Her eyes opened. She looked at him but didn't seem to really see him. She looked around the room, and winced when she moved her head, then closed her eyes again.

"Meghan?"

But she had already gone back to wherever she had come from.

Cavan went back to his chair and sank down into it. Paddy walked quietly in. "Anything?"

Cavan glanced up at him. "She woke for a moment, but she didn't say anything."

"Well, at least it's something. Would you like me to sit for a while?"

"No, thank you. I want to stay with her."

"Can I send you some dinner?"

"No."

"All right. Call me if you need me."

Meggie grew more restless as the night progressed. Twice Cavan had to restrain her to keep her from tearing off the sling. When it was almost morning,

Cavan left the chair to poke at the dying fire, then walked to the window to stretch and look outside.

"Cavan?"

He moved quickly back to the bed and looked down at her. Meggie's eyes were open and this time when she looked at him, she really saw him. "Good morning."

"What am I doing at Grandfather's?"

He smoothed her hair away from her forehead and smiled down at her. "I brought you here after the accident."

"What accident?"

He looked at her curiously. "What's the last thing you remember?"

Meggie thought for a minute. "We came home from the ball. You had to make a phone call and I waited for you upstairs. Then you came to me and said you had to go to New York, but you'd be back the next day."

"You don't remember anything after that?"

She shook her head and gasped at the pain that shot through her, and when she tried to lift her arm to touch her head, that hurt, too. "What happened?"

He took her hand in his and held it. "You were riding a horse when you were shot in the shoulder. It knocked you from the horse, and when you fell you hit your head on a rock."

"Shot? I was shot? By whom?"

"Hugh Farrell."

Meggie looked at him in amazement. "Why?"

"Because of me. I took away everything he cherished. He wanted to do the same to me. How do you feel?"

Meggie smiled at him. "Like I got shot in the shoulder and hit my head on a rock."

Cavan shook his head and tenderly touched her cheek. "It's good to have you back."

"Such as I am."

"Such as you are. Can I get you anything?"

"Food. I'm famished."

"How about some broth?"

Meggie wrinkled her nose.

"My sentiments exactly, but I'm afraid you're stuck with that for a few days."

She smiled wearily, and closed her eyes again. "I'm so tired. Hungry, but tired."

"Then go back to sleep," he said softly. "I'll have something here for you to eat when you wake. And Meghan?"

She opened her eyes.

"I love you."

There was no smile this time as she looked into his eyes. "You told me that when I was unconscious, didn't you?"

"Yes."

"I heard you. And I love you, too." Her eyes drifted closed.

Cavan took a deep breath as he watched her sleep.

When her grandfather came into the room, Cavan rose from the bed and signaled for him to go back into the hall. Cavan followed him and closed the door. "She's asleep now, but she's conscious. She doesn't remember what happened."

"Not any of it?"

"Nothing about you or me. Her last memory is of my leaving for New York the night before this happened."

"What do we do? Should we tell her?"

"Not telling her is what got us into trouble in the first place. I think we should tell her, but not until she's better."

"All right. I'll follow your lead on this."

"I'd appreciate it if you'd sit with her for a while. I want to go back where she was shot and look for the bullet."

"It's a long shot, if you'll pardon the expression."

Cavan smiled at him. "My long shots paying off are what made me famous. I'll be back later."

Paddy went quietly into the room and watched Meggie sleep. He couldn't help but think that if he'd just been honest with her in the beginning, none of this would have happened.

Cavan took one of Padraic's horses and rode it to the exact spot where Meggie had fallen. For more than five hours he was on his hands and knees searching through the leaves and grass. Every square foot, inch by slow, methodical inch.

And then he found it.

Unsmiling, he sat back on his heels and studied it. The doctor had been right. It was small caliber.

"Got'cha, Farrell."

Chapter Ten

As Meggie sat on her own bed five days after the shooting, the doctor removed her sling. "Show me how high you can lift your arm before it hurts." Meggie raised her arm about shoulder high and winced. "That's it."

"I think we'll just leave the sling off now. You need to use your arm. Try to lift it higher every day, but expect it to hurt for another two weeks or so. How's your head?"

"Fine. I still have a little lump, but I'm not as dizzy as I was."

He patted her good shoulder. "As I said, another two weeks and you'll be back in fighting form. Where's your husband?"

"Downstairs."

"I'll give him the good word before I go. I understand that Hugh Farrell has been indicted for attempted murder."

"That's right."

He shook his head as he rose and picked up his medical bag. "Strange how things work out sometimes."

When he had gone, Meggie got up and walked to the window. It was a beautiful day out. Sean was near the stables working with the horses that had arrived from America the day before. He saw her in the window and armed her a big wave. She waved back. He was as much humiliated as grieved over what his father had done.

Arms suddenly slid around her waist, pulling her back against a strong, lean body. Meggie relaxed against Cavan and tilted her head back. "Good morning."

"How are you feeling?"

"I'm all healed."

"That's not what the doctor says."

"All right. I'm almost all healed."

"I had someone bring your car back from the orphanage. I don't want you driving for a few more days though. If you need something, tell me and I'll get it for you."

Meggie turned in his arms. "All I need is to get back to normal. I want to start our life together."

He kissed her forehead and held her close. "I know."

She paused, gathering her courage. "I want us to adopt Sarah."

"I know that, too. I've already spoken with the orphanage, and in the words of one of the nuns, they'll get back to us."

Meggie beamed up at him. "Thank you."

"You don't need to thank me. A person would have to be a stone not to want to adopt Sarah." He looked at his watch. "I have to meet someone. I'll be back in a few hours."

Meggie reached up and lightly touched her mouth to his. "Goodbye."

The grooves in his cheeks deepened. "You're a very difficult woman to leave."

"Then stay."

"I can't. This is important to both of us. I'll tell you about it when I get back."

Millie came into the bedroom with a breakfast tray just as Cavan was leaving. "Where's he off to?" she asked as she set it down on a table next to the bed.

"I don't know, but he won't be gone long." Meggie eyed the tray. "Would you mind if I ate downstairs? I'm beginning to feel like an invalid."

"Of course not." She straightened out the bedclothes. "I'm so glad everything is turning out the way it is. I'll tell you, after the things that Pierson woman said to you, and the way you ran out of here, I didn't think you'd ever be back with your husband."

Meggie looked at her curiously. "What things?"

"Oh, you know, about your grandfather being the one who put Cavan in prison."

Meggie just stared at the housekeeper without really seeing her. She was seeing Jessica Pierson standing in the library. She was hearing what she'd said. And the same horror that had washed over her then, washed over her now.

"Meggie?"

She focused on the housekeeper.

"Are you all right?"

"What?"

"I asked if you were all right?"

"Yes. I'm fine, Millie. But I've changed my mind about breakfast. I'm not really hungry. Would you just take it away, please?"

Millie eyed her worriedly as she picked up the tray and left. Meggie sank onto the side of the bed and just sat there, her hands clasped tightly in her lap. How could she have forgotten that?

Rising slowly, Meggie walked to the small desk in a corner of the room and pulled out a pen and some stationery.

Dear Cavan, I've gone off somewhere to be alone and think. Please don't worry about me. I'll be fine.

                                        Meggie.

She propped it up against a lamp and with a calm that surprised her, packed some things in a suitcase. It wasn't very heavy, but Meggie was still weak. She carried it out of her room and had to stop to rest. Then she managed a few steps and had to stop again.

Millie walked past the bottom of the stairs then turned back and looked up at her. "What are you doing?"

"Taking this to my car."

"You're doing no such thing." She stormed up and tried to take it from Meggie, but Meggie held on to it.

"Look, Millie, if you don't want to help me, go away so I can do it myself."

"You're in no condition to drive."

"I'm in no condition to walk. Driving is the easy part."

Millie looked at her for a long moment. "I'll carry it to the car for you, but I want to go on record as saying that I don't like this. Not a bit. I don't know what your husband will say when he gets home."

They walked down the stairs together, and then Meggie climbed behind the steering wheel. Sean came running across the lawn and leaned in the car window. "Where are you going?"

"I'll tell you where she *should* be going," Millie told him. "Back to bed. Straight back to bed."

He looked at Meggie. "Where are you going?" he asked again, quietly.

"To my cottage."

"You're in no condition to drive that far, Meggie."

"I need to be alone."

He opened the car door. "Get out."

"Sean . . ."

"I'm going to drive you. Get in the passenger side."

"But . . ."

"Don't argue with me. You'll waste a lot of energy and lose in the end anyway."

Meggie climbed out of the car and walked around to the passenger side while Sean started the engine. As Meggie closed the door, he looked over at her. "Ready?"

She nodded.

He put the car into gear and they drove off with Millie, hands on hips, shaking her head behind them.

Sean looked over at Meggie as she settled back against the seat and closed her eyes. "Do you want to talk?"

"No."

"All right." And not another word passed between them on the drive.

Four hours later Sean stopped in front of a very old, whitewashed, vine-covered cottage. It only had two rooms, and it sat perched back on the cliffs overlooking the North Sea.

"I'll drive your car home and then come back for you in a few days," Sean said.

"All right." She climbed out and took a deep breath of the fresh air while Sean took her suitcase from the trunk and carried it into the unlocked cottage.

When he came back out, she was still standing there. "Do you need any groceries?"

She shook her head. "I'll walk into town and buy a few things later." Meggie managed a smile. "Thank you for bringing me."

He gave her a light hug. "If you need anything, call."

"I will."

He climbed back into the car and Meggie was alone. She walked down the flower-lined cobbled walk to the bright green front door. The interior was white, with wood floors and handwoven scatter rugs. The furniture was old-fashioned, large and dark, but lovely.

The kitchen was an old one with few modern conveniences, but cheerful, with a large wooden table in the middle. There was a tiny bedroom with just enough room for the feather bed and storage trunk in front of it, and an armoire for her clothes. The bathroom also was tiny with an ancient, footed tub.

There was no heating system in the cottage other than the large fireplaces in both the living room and bedroom, and as the chill of the afternoon settled over her little home, Meggie added fuel to the fires until they burned brightly.

Then she sat in a chair wrapped in a blanket and stared into the flames.

Meggie still didn't remember being shot, but she remembered every word Jessica had said to her, and she remembered every word she had said to her grandfather.

And Cavan. How could he look at her and not hate her for what her grandfather had done?

Where did she go from here?

Meggie spent the next few days sleeping a lot. Every day she grew stronger. She spent time working with her flowers, and a lot of time sitting on the cliffs. She knew she had some problems to face when she got back home, but for now she had outer if not inner peace.

On the afternoon of her fourth day there, the sun hadn't shone all day. Meggie walked out to the cliffs in a long, full skirt and sweater, a wool shawl wrapped around her shoulders, and stood staring out to sea. The wind whipped her long auburn hair behind her. She didn't hear the car drive up, nor did she see Cavan standing near it, watching her in the distance.

When Meggie turned to walk back to the house, she smiled at the sight of the car. Sean was back. And she was ready to go home. She pushed open the front door and hung her shawl on a wooden hook. "Sean?"

When there was no answer, she walked farther into the living room. "Sean?"

Cavan stepped out of the bedroom. "Hello, Meghan."

Her startled eyes flew to his face. "What are you doing here?"

"You've had your time alone. Now we need to talk."

"There isn't all that much to say."

"I think there is. Millie told me what she said to you the morning you left. I take it you remembered the rest of your conversation with Jessica on your own."

"My grandfather sent you to prison."

"That's right."

"Why didn't you tell me? Why didn't he tell me?"

"May I sit down?"

Meggie waved him into a chair and she sat on a footstool near the fireplace. "I didn't tell you at first because it wasn't necessary, and later because I knew it would hurt you. Your grandfather didn't tell you because he hoped you'd never have to know."

"You married me out of hatred for my grandfather."

Cavan said nothing.

"When I agreed to marry you, I thought that your anger was directed at someone else entirely, not my family. If I'd known how personal it was, I would have known then you could never fall in love with me."

"But I did."

"Are you saying that when you look at me, you don't see an O'Neill?"

"I used to. It was a problem for me. But not anymore. And even if I did, it wouldn't matter. I don't hate your grandfather anymore. He did what he had to."

Meggie rose abruptly. "Cavan, I thought I was ready to talk about this, but I'm not."

"We have to, Meggie, or we'll never be able to start our lives. Hugh Farrell was furious when I ran off with Caroline. He was in financial trouble even then, and he was counting on Caroline's dowry to bail him out. When I ran off with her, he planted the jewels in the cottage I had and then forced your grandfather to lie about seeing me with the jewels with the threat that you would be harmed if he didn't. You have to see that to your grandfather there was no choice between the two of us. He couldn't let anything happen to you."

"He should have called the police."

"And what could they have done? Slapped Hugh on the wrist and let him go, leaving your grandfather to deal with him as best he could, worrying about you whenever you were out of his sight for more than a few minutes. If I can understand why he did what he did, why can't you?"

Meggie turned away from him. "I can understand it." A shiver went through her. "Oh, Cavan, the things I said to him."

He came up behind her and placed his hands on her arms, but she moved away from him. "Don't, please, Cavan. As I said, I do understand why he lied, but it doesn't really change anything, does it? This will always be something between us."

"What are you saying?"

"I want an annulment. I want you to be able to have a wife you marry out of love, and I want a husband who, when he's angry with me, won't leave me wondering if there isn't still some deep resentment."

"No."

She turned and looked at him with surprised eyes. "I'm not your possession."

Cavan stood in front of her and cupped her face in his hands. His mouth came to rest on hers with a tenderness that left an ache deep within her. "But you are, Meghan. Just as I'm yours. The only man you're going to live with is me." His hand touched her hair. "The only man who's ever going to make love to you is me, just as you're the only woman I'll ever make love to." His eyes gazed into hers. "The only man you'll ever love is me, just as the only woman I'll ever love is you. We belong together, and we're going to be together."

A tear trailed down her cheek, and Cavan kissed it.

"I've done some things over the past few weeks that will give us a fresh start. I've sold the company I owned that competed with your grandfather's. He'll be on solid ground now. And I've arranged to turn the estate I won from Hugh Farrell over to Sean. It really belongs to him anyway."

Another tear dropped down Meggie's cheek. "Thank you."

"But we'll be staying there until our new house is finished."

"Our new house?"

"On the land I bought."

"You want to live in Ireland?"

"Somehow I can't picture you anywhere else."

"You won't be bored?"

"Living with you is hardly conducive to boredom, Meghan." He gazed deeply into her eyes. "I love you. I've never in my life said that to another human being. You're like some miracle to me. If you walk out of my life, there'll be nothing left."

Meggie moved into his arms and Cavan held her tightly to him. All of a sudden she wondered how she could ever have considered leaving him.

"There's something in the bedroom I'd like you to put on."

She moved a little away from him. "What is it?"

"Don't ask questions. Just put it on and meet me out here in front of the fireplace in ten minutes."

She looked at him curiously, but did as she was told.

"Close the door behind you," Cavan called as she walked into the bedroom.

Meggie did, then sank onto the edge of the bed and fingered the rich material of her wedding dress that Cavan had laid on the bed. "Oh, Cavan," she whispered.

With a happy heart, she slipped out of the clothes she had on and put on the dress. She couldn't do her hair up again because she still couldn't lift her arm high enough, so she just brushed it until it shone.

There was a knock on the bedroom door and Meggie answered it. Cavan's eyes told her all she needed to know about the way she looked. And he had changed into a tuxedo.

He held out his arm and Meggie put her hand lightly on it as he escorted her into the living room. It was dark outside. Cavan had built up the fire a little and lit some candles. There were flowers.

He took her to a spot in front of the fire and helped her to kneel on a pillow, then he kneeled on one in front of her and took her hands in his as he gazed into her eyes.

"I know what a disappointment our first wedding was to you."

When she would have protested he touched his fingers to her mouth.

"I, Cavan Gallagher, take you, Meghan Kathleen O'Neill Gallagher to be my wife. To love and cherish for as long as we live." He gently squeezed her hands.

"Now, it's your turn. I, Meghan Kathleen O'Neill Gallagher..."

"I, Meghan Kathleen O'Neill Gallagher," she repeated.

"Take you, Cavan Gallagher..."

"Take you, Cavan Gallagher."

"To be my husband. To..."

Now Meggie touched her fingers to his mouth. "To be my husband," she said in almost a whisper. "To love and cherish for as long as we live."

Cavan reached into his pocket and brought out a square cut emerald ring. He raised her left hand and kissed her finger before sliding on the ring. "I now pronounce us husband and wife."

Meggie just kneeled there looking at him.

He reached out a gentle hand and cupped her face. "Are you going to cry again?"

She nodded.

"You seem to be doing a lot of that lately."

She nodded again.

He leaned toward her and rested his mouth gently on hers. When he felt her lips tremble, he wrapped her in his arms. Meggie strained her body toward him, unable to get close enough, burying her face in his neck.

Cavan put his hand on the back of her head, and tightly closed his eyes. He would never have believed it was possible to love someone as much as he loved Meggie. He couldn't imagine a life without her.

Meggie moved slightly away from him and gazed into his eyes. She wanted him as much as he wanted her. Their desire vibrated in the room. Meggie reached behind her and silently lowered the hidden zipper of her dress. With her arms crossed over her breasts, she slowly pulled the dress from her shoulders and let it drop to her waist as she kneeled before him.

Cavan leaned forward and kissed the side of her neck and along her shoulder to the gentle curve of her breast. Meggie closed her eyes and tilted her head back when his mouth found her nipple and gently suckled. Her fingers tangled in his hair, drawing him closer.

Suddenly he moved away from her, his eyes still on hers as he took off his jacket and shirt. Meggie loved Cavan's strong body, and when he lowered her to the rug and pressed his chest against her breasts, she wrapped her arms around him and held him closer.

Piece by piece their clothing fell away until they lay there naked. Cavan looked down at her in the glow of the firelight and trailed his fingers down her thigh. "You're beautiful."

His hand came back up along the inside of her smooth thigh as his tongue explored her ear. When his fingers found their goal, Meggie stiffened for a moment. Cavan grew still until she relaxed, and gently he began caressing her.

The warmth that had been growing in her spread, and a tension started growing low in her stomach. Suddenly Meggie wasn't thinking anymore. She was only feeling. Feeling what he was doing to her with every movement, every kiss. She was straining against him, searching for the fulfillment she instinctively knew was so close at hand.

Cavan moved on top of her with the gentleness of a man in love.

Meggie's eyes flew open. Cavan remained still as he gazed down at her, pushing her damp hair away from her forehead. Then he began to move, slowly, rhythmically thrusting deeper and deeper.

The same tension she had felt before began building in Meggie again. Her fingers dug into his shoulders, pulling his body more tightly to hers. It was so close.

Suddenly an explosion seemed to go off inside her and she couldn't move anymore as it rocked through her whole body. She lay there limply as Cavan gazed down at her, then she started to tremble. Cavan stood up and lifted her in his arms as he carried her to the bed and laid her beneath the blankets. Then he got in next to her and pulled her into his arms. "Are you all right?"

She nodded against his shoulder. "I wasn't expecting it to be like that."

Cavan rubbed his cheek against her hair. "I wasn't either," he said in a voice thick with emotion.

Meggie turned slightly and raised on an elbow so that she could look at him.

He touched her face with a gentle hand and then pulled her back to his shoulder. "Don't ever leave me, Meggie."

An overwhelming feeling of contentment filled her heart. There was no mistaking how Cavan felt about her. There were no shadows any longer. She was Cavan Gallagher's lady. Cavan Gallagher's wife in the truest sense of that word.

And nothing else mattered.

Silhouette Romance

COMING NEXT MONTH

RELUCTANT DREAMER—Dixie Browning
Her son and her gift shop were Portia's whole life, until Cole Randolph showed up. They clashed at every turn, but neither wanted to deny the love growing between them.

YESTERDAY ONCE MORE—Debbie Macomber
The most difficult decision Julie had ever made was to leave Kansas. But her heart demanded that she return and fight for Daniel's love.

LADY OF THE WEST—Jennifer Mikels
Her authentic frontier town was in trouble, so Tory advertised for help. Enter stage left: actor Josh Bannion, former cinema sex symbol. Enter stage right: love.

LOVE BUG—Kat Adams
After slaughtering Kelley's snapdragons, thirteen-year-old J. T. Landers came up with the perfect idea: fix Kelley up with his widowed father, Jason. His willing partner in crime—Kelley's daughter, Leigh.

JUST ONE LOOK—Jude O'Neill
Their relationship was a fast-paced thirties comedy film. Could Zan and Stu's love survive icy dunkings in San Francisco Bay and three cheerfully interfering old women? Sure—after a muddy, slippery bicycle ride.

LAS VEGAS MATCH—Barbara Turner
Jenna was determined to save her sister from that ruthless man, so she tricked Kirby Carmichael into ''marrying'' her. What she didn't know was that their ''phony'' marriage was real—and that Kirby had no intention of telling her.

AVAILABLE THIS MONTH:

Silhouette Desire

Available
October 1986

California
Copper

The second in an exciting new
Desire Trilogy by Joan Hohl.

If you fell in love with Thackery—the
laconic charmer of *Texas Gold*—you're
sure to feel the same about his twin
brother, Zackery.

In *California Copper*, Zackery meets the
beautiful Aubrey Mason on the windswept
Pacific coast. Tormented by memories,
Aubrey has only to trust . . . to embrace
Zack's flame . . . and he can ignite the fire in
her heart.

The trilogy continues when you
meet Kit Aimsley, the twins' half
sister, in *Nevada Silver*. Look for
Nevada Silver—coming soon from
Silhouette Books.

SIL-SE-1RR

Take 4 Silhouette Special Edition novels
FREE
and preview future books in your home for 15 days!

When you take advantage of this offer, you get 4 Silhouette Special Edition® novels FREE and without obligation. Then you'll also have the opportunity to preview 6 brand-new books —delivered right to your door for a FREE 15-day examination period—as soon as they are published.

When you decide to keep them, you pay just $1.95 each ($2.50 each in Canada) *with no shipping, handling, or other charges of any kind!*

Romance *is* alive, well and flourishing in the moving love stories of Silhouette Special Edition novels. They'll awaken your desires, enliven your senses, and leave you tingling all over with excitement...and the first 4 novels are yours to keep. You can cancel at any time.

As an added bonus, you'll also receive a FREE subscription to the Silhouette Books Newsletter as long as you remain a member. Each issue is filled with news on upcoming books, interviews with your favorite authors, even their favorite recipes.

To get your 4 FREE books, fill out and mail the coupon today!

Silhouette Special Edition®

Silhouette Books, 120 Brighton Rd., P.O. Box 5084, Clifton, NJ 07015-5084

**Clip and mail to: Silhouette Books,
120 Brighton Road, P.O. Box 5084, Clifton, NJ 07015-5084** •

YES. Please send me 4 FREE Silhouette Special Edition novels. Unless you hear from me after I receive them, send me 6 new Silhouette Special Edition novels to preview each month. I understand you will bill me just $1.95 each, a total of $11.70 (in Canada, $2.50 each, a total of $15.00), with no shipping, handling, or other charges of any kind. There is no minimum number of books that I must buy, and I can cancel at any time. The first 4 books are mine to keep.

BS18R6

Name _____ (please print)

Address _____ Apt. #

City _____ State/Prov. _____ Zip/Postal Code

* In Canada, mail to: Silhouette Canadian Book Club, 320 Steelcase Rd., E.,
Markham, Ontario, L3R 2M1, Canada
Terms and prices subject to change.
SILHOUETTE SPECIAL EDITION is a service mark and registered trademark.   SE-SUB-1